Never Fall for the Stuntman

To meat –
Live your dreams!
xoxo
[illegible]

Never Fall for the Stuntman

A Novel

Jennifer Shortridge

iUniverse, Inc.
New York Lincoln Shanghai

Never Fall for the Stuntman

iUniverse books may be ordered through booksellers or by contacting:

iUniverse
2021 Pine Lake Road, Suite 100
Lincoln, NE 68512
www.iuniverse.com
1-800-Authors (1-800-288-4677)

ISBN: 978-0-595-46499-9 (pbk)

ISBN: 978-0-595-90797-7 (ebk)

Printed in the United States of America

To Rich, in an impressive instant you lit my inspiration wick.

Thanks for being so damn sexy.

"What the hell am I doing up here?" she said aloud. Fifteen stories up and standing on the edge of a building, the harness around her waist closing in like a cage. Every shallow breath she took felt like a vice grip squeezing her ribs up into her throat. Gasping for air, her lungs heaving, Jenna tried to slow her breathing. With one last look at the hundred or so foot descent, her stomach flopped like a fish out of water despite her bravado. Stunt school had prepared her and Jenna trained hard, but no one told her how frightening it would really be.

"Action!" A megaphone voice shouted to her.

Did he just say action? Am I really about to leap off this building with a half-inch wire and harness holding me? Maybe this will finally get his attention. I am either going to plunge my death ... or pull off the coolest stunt ever. Here you go, Mr. Six-Pack abs. I hope you are impressed, Jenna thought as she inched slowly to the building edge. In less than ten seconds, she would be hero or zero.

Placing one leg over the ledge, and a small footstep later, Jenna plunged off the building graceful as an angel descending from the clouds. The cable whirred in her ear like the world's loudest zipper, blasting her eardrums, deafening her.

Amazingly, Jenna kept her eyes open the entire ride to the earth. Ten short feet from the ground the wire pulleys ground to a quick halt, knocking the wind from her lungs.

"Cut! Print. Perfect shot. Get her down." The director shouted.

"Can't ... breathe," she huffed, still suspended in air. All she could hear was the sound of muffled clapping before everything went dark.

"Jen!" A man's voice called out to her.

Shaking her head to clear the fogginess, Jenna spoke. "Wuh? Did I make the shot?"

"You blacked out," the man said as his face became clear.

Looking at Scotty Perelli, an extremely hunky thirty-two year-old stunt coordinator and her personal mentor, she smiled. He took her arm and helped her sit up.

"We got it, good job." He grinned as he checked her for bruises.

The blood rushed to her head as Scotty lifted her from the ground and made Jenna wobble to get her balance. She looked around to see if the object of her mad desire was watching her first high-flying stunt. Through the slew of actors, extras, grips, and crew, she spotted him; the reason she was there. The sexiest hunk of a man Jenna ever set eyes on, first on film and then in person, lead actor and stunt professional, Rock Constantine.

One tall drink o'water. *Oh my god, oh my god, he is walking over this way, Shit! He is heading right towards me. Be cool and try not to look like a deer in headlights.* Smoothing down her long blonde ponytail, Jenna tried to look away casually but froze and stared directly at him. His intense gaze burned her like a hot knife though butter.

He's staring at me! Smile, look cute, she told herself. Rock walked directly at her—and then right around her, not even acknowledging she existed. Rock went to Scotty, and began discussing the shot. Jenna's mouth fell open and she stared in shock. I just nearly killed myself trying to impress this man and he does not even notice me! She chided herself for not making the move to speak. Watching the two men discussing the next upcoming stunt, Jenna jammed her gear and safety equipment into her hot pink duffle bag, straining to hear the conversation. Her heart pounded; the object of her fascination and lust stood barely five feet away from her.

Standing at least six-three, maybe six-four, Rock was a tall, lean wall of muscles. Finely shaped shoulders and long arms bulged out of the army green wife beater that clung to his well-toned and long torso. Jenna stared at his long black hair captured into a tight ponytail that accented his high cheekbones. Dark, piercing brown eyes gave him an air of mystery. Years of stunt training, martial arts and physical preparation chiseled his body to the most beautifully cut, statue-of-a-god physique. She spent hours trying to figure out his nationality. Native American? Black? Irish? Italian? His fair skin did nothing to help her question. *Who cares*, she thought. *He is hunk with a capital H!*

A full five inches shorter was Scotty, Italian stallion. Equally gorgeous and athletic, Scotty was the kindest, most caring person Jenna had ever met. Scotty took Jenna under his wing and mentored her when she enrolled in his stunt school. He truly believed she had a talent for this line of work and encouraged her to do this film for her first real job.

I wish Rock would take off his shirt, she thought as she sighed and looked him up and down in one long glance. Jenna had seen that smoking hot body on film but really wanted to get a full view in the Southern California sunshine, or maybe just in his trailer. Grinning naughtily, Jenna faded into a daydream of nicely wicked things she would like to do to her stuntman in bed. Lost in her days dream, she felt rather self-conscience when she realized he was staring. Jenna snapped out of her fantasy and looked up from her crouched position to see Rock watching her strangely. They locked eyes as he walked past Jenna, and he spoke to her for the first time.

"Good job, kiddo."

She smiled and stood. "Thanks Mr. Constantine".

With a look over his shoulder, the hunky man winked. "Call me Rock".

"Okay Mr. Rock." Jenna stumbled over her tongue, which had suddenly become thick.

He gave a small sneer as he turned and walked away.

"Bye," she said quietly, slipping back into her daydream.

"Jen, Jen!"

She spun around. "Huh?"

"Next shot. We need to hustle." Scotty yelled, pointing his thumb.

Jenna's five-foot frame was the perfect stand in for the pop-star-turned actress, Missy Manga and her long blonde tresses matched the stick-figure girl's expensively treated color. While setting up the next scene they had Jenna stand in the same position for over an hour as the lighting, camera, sound and other departments set up shots. Her legs cramped tightly but she stayed statue still. It's so unfair! Ten million to shoot a bimbo who cannot act worth crap and I am making squat. Life is so imbalanced. *No*, its not she told herself. *You are here because you want to be here—to meet Rock, have an adventure, and hopefully get laid!*

Stepping into the scene, Rock walked to the mark next to her. *What is going on?* She thought as his towering presence shaded her small body and made her quiver.

"Okay, now lean over so we can get the angle for the kiss," Jared, the fresh-faced director barked. Panic flooded her. *What kiss? How's my breath? What did I eat for breakfast?* Questions troubled her mind buy they tumbled away as he leaned over and placed his soft lips on hers. *I've died and gone to …*

His hands slid over her jaw and he released his hot mouth from hers. Head swimming, Jenna opened her eyes slowly, with a breathy sigh, and was taken aback to find him looking deeply into her face.

"Okay we got it," Jared snapped. And just like that, Rock walked away, a ghost disappearing into the night. Jenna stood, open-mouthed in stunned disbelief.

"I just kissed Rock," she whispered to no one.

"Bring in Missy," someone shouted.

Missy Manga—teen pop star who had one synthesized pop hit six months ago, walked on stage as if her shit did not stink. Bleached-blonde hair extensions, over caked make up, white veneers; size zero, no talent … and nineteen. No money in the world could make her remember one stinking line. The "Pop Tart", as Jenna and her new on-set friend Tracy liked to refer to her, approached and yelling out orders to the crew.

"Like, can someone get me a fucking diet soda or what?" Missy barked.

With a wave, Missy dismissed Jenna and she was released from the-statue like posture. The actress, if you could call her that, took her mark. A moment later, the man-hunk of Jenna's dreams strode in to shoot the scene.

"Gimme my line!" the pop tart demanded loudly.

"You cannot be serious," Jenna uttered under her breath. "She only has to say like, ten words and she can't remember them?"

Missy's assistant called to the actress. It took nearly ten takes for her to get her line right. Then it happened; Rock stepped in and kissed the pop tart just as he had kissed Jenna earlier. Her heart felt as if it dropped to her feet and broke in a million pieces. Crushed, Jenna sighed to herself. He was just acting. Our kiss meant nothing.

"Cut." The assistant director shouted as Jenna sank back further into the crew as Rock walked off set with an assistant behind him. The pop princess flipped open her cell phone as she walked right in front of Jenna.

"Oh my god, I just totally had to do a kissing scene, he's like old enough to be my dad! But he is an awesome kisser." Missy said, moving off the set.

Old! Jenna fumed at the pop tart. He's not even ten years older than her or me.

Back at the tent that was set up for the lowest of the crew's food chain, Jenna entered and took a seat on the folding chair next to her cot. The view was perfectly in line with Rock's trailer—and not a bit coincidental.

Staring at the mid-size white trailer that housed the man with the perfect body, face, and who starred in most all of her fantasies, Jenna slid off her boots. Rock entered the trailer and slammed the door. *Wait! I need another chance to see him today*. Maybe and if Jenna played her cards right, she could get him to help her with the next fight-scene rehearsal. She laid her tired, bruised body on the cot and closed her eyes. I'll have him in my dreams. Just as she drifted off, daydreaming of being ravished by Rock, someone called her name and snapped her back into reality.

"Jenna, Jen!"

"Sorry," she said, blushing fiercely. "I was going over the fight-scene steps in my mind."

"Sure you were. You were watching that trailer. Come on, let's get lunch."

Tracy, an 'extra' who had befriended Jenna on the first day of shooting, dragged her up from the chair and out into the California sunshine. Tracy was perky, super inquisitive, a girl-next door transplant from Florida who was sleeping with the director's brother; a feat that secured her a bit part in the film they were shooting.

Strolling arm in arm, the two friends entered the catering tent, laughing about the pop-tart's acting abilities. Cardboard had more expressions. The less-than-stellar actress was quickly forgotten as they spotted food.

"Oh, mashed potatoes! Want some?" Tracy asked.

"No, I can't even gain two pounds. I won't be able to fit in the cat suit for the next scene." Opting for cottage cheese and salad with no dressing, Jenna choked it down, imagining it was a juicy Fat Burger. The girlfriends sat and swapped stories, gossip before Tracy laughed and nudged Jenna.

Tracy grinned wickedly. "There's your man."

"Where?" Jenna whipped her head around.

"In the chow line," Tracy said.

Rock stood in front of the buffet, deciding what to eat.

"I'd like a slice of him with whipped cream," Tracy quipped.

"Back off, he's my fantasy!" The two giggled like silly schoolchildren staring at Adonis.

"Don't look now," Tracy said.

"What?" Jenna gasped. She locked eyes with Rock.

"Oh my god, he's coming right this way."

Jenna winced. "Don't say coming."

"Hey," he said casually.

"Hey, Rock," Jenna said.

Rock looked past her as if she did not exist.

"What's up, man?" A male voice sounded from behind the two women. She realized he was not talking to her at all but to another stunt extra.

"I have to get out of here." Jenna gripped her friend by the arm and pulled her out of the tent. "I feel like an idiot. I am so mortified!" Jenna slapped her hand to her forehead.

Tracy rolled her blue eyes. "Come back after the dinner break. I want to show you my new shoes."

"Okay, see ya tramp!" Jenna joked.

"Bye Slut!" Tracy yelled back and ran.

Later, after reporting to the stunt coordinators tent, Jenna took a seat to wait as Scotty finished talking to a production assistant on his two-way radio. He spotted her and yelled, "We'll be ready in twenty minutes ... Jen, run to wardrobe, and get in the outfit for the ninja fight scene".

"We're shooting it today? I thought we had two more days to prepare!"

"Change of plans. We will make it up as we go along. Go!"

Without hesitation, she jumped up and ran across the set like O.J. in an airport.

In six minutes flat, she was poured into the skin-tight red latex cat suit and matching spike stiletto-heeled boots. She pulled her long blonde hair into a ponytail high on her head, applied false eyelashes, and painted her lips a bright, flame red. Catcalls and whistles came from every direction as she approached the set on the back lot designed to look like a futuristic Chinatown alley.

I'm glad I had cottage cheese for lunch, she thought, holding in her stomach. Jenna's size four frame felt molded into the rubbery suit. Scotty and another technician blinked and had to adjust themselves discreetly as her ample size C's filled the suit to perfection.

"Put your tongues back in your mouths, you wolves." She grinned mockingly.

Scotty blushed as he placed the rigging over her chest for the high-flying fight.

As he went over all the safety checks with her, the Pop Tart approached with her dotting assistant. In the matching cat suit, the size zero Missy looked hideously anorexic, her bones sticking out like a starving refugee.

"Make her take those out," the actress demanded as she pointed to Jenna's boobs.

"Excuse me?" Jenna stammered. "They're real, and if I take them out I would be arrested for indecent exposure".

Scotty grabbed her arm and pulled her aside. "Don't piss off the diva please, we all need this job to go as smooth as possible so we can get through this shoot and get paid."

"Sorry … they are real." Jenna protested as he looked at her chest and raised his eyebrows twice.

"Okay, so this is the scene; you're meeting the Asian nemesis. Just do some basic karate or judo moves and follow Rock's lead." The director sat with a chart on his lap.

"Rock? I'm fighting with Rock?" She asked Scotty who ignored her, busying himself with watching the camera monitor.

"On marks please, everyone." A voice boomed instructions before Jenna had a chance to be nervous.

"Oh boy!" Jenna sighed as she stepped into place. To the left she saw the young teenager Missy flirting with her sexy sparing partner, smiling and touching his arm. Rock left the starlet and stepped on to his position. Jenna fumed as the pop tart gave Jenna a bitchy smirk. Coming over to give her quick directions, Jared the director told them, "Let's start with a few swings and punches, then Jenna—I need you to high kick as close to Rock's face as possible."

Let's do it. Jenna dared one last look at Rock. Missy winked at him. He ignored it as he went into serious action mode.

"Unfuckingbelievable." Jenna said under her breath.

"Ready?" Rock asked her.

"Are you?" Jenna replied snidely as she stretched her neck both ways and prepared her stance.

"Action," the director shouted and Jenna unleashed her frustrations. Adrenaline kicked in to high gear as Jenna went after Rock with force and intensity, throwing precise arms chops. Rock's perfect timing and response to her actions gracefully thwarted each blow. Suddenly, a strong arm grabbed her, spinning her round such that his tall lean body clung tightly to her back. Her heart pounded as she felt the heat from his bulk through the latex suit. With one leg kick straight up next to her ear, she went for his face.

Lucky his reflexes were so good, Rock thought as he ducked his head to avoid the pointy toe of the boot into his eye. Spinning around, Jenna went after him full throttle, and Rock went from paid actor to real fighter. Each lunge and swing became more aggressive and real.

She could sense he was really getting into it as Jenna grew angrier and went blazing with the kicks, taking out her aggression on him. They moved around as she caught him off guard and kicked his legs out from under him. *Shit! That was rough, I am so fired,* she thought, not realizing she was smirking at him.

How did I not see that coming, he thought. Rock growled; her expression irritated him and he released some frustration of his own. Neither of them heard the director call cut. He pounced and twisted her legs between his ankles, dropping her to the floor. First falling down together and quickly rolling off each other, both Rock and Jenna stood before lunging at each other viciously.

Sharp as a razor's edge, the tension sliced the air between them. Jenna took her shoulder, rammed it into his gut, and kicked his legs out from under him. He fell to the ground with a sound thud. The crew stood silent as they all watched the two go after each other with fury. This time he let her think she got one over on him, but he knew what he was doing—controlling every move. Rock let her tackle him to the ground. As they fell to the hard dirt floor, Jenna landed directly on top of his sweaty body. Straddling his chest, her knees on his shoulders, she looked down at him in hard-earned victory. In one quick movement, Rock grabbed both of her wrists, flipped her over onto her back, and pinned her down hard to the floor. She was trapped as he held her arms high over her head. Panting like a lioness in the desert sun, her chest heaved as she gasped for breath. Jenna stared furiously at him. Rock kept his face emotionless as Jenna stared up at him angrily. Holding her still, Rock bore down his hips, locking them over hers. His growing bulge pressing down onto her, Jenna felt sharp pangs of excitement between her legs, sending her libido skyrocketing.

"That's a wrap for now," The director quipped.

The buzz of adrenaline filled her ears as someone yelled cut but Rock did not release her right away. The weight of him crushing down on her body felt so damn good. She begged him silently not to stop, even as she squirmed to get free. The more she squirmed the tighter he held her down, trapped between his bulging member and the ground. Without a word, he took a minute to compose himself and his hard-on before he released her and stood up. Circulation was nearly cut off in her hands and they felt like a thousand pinpricks, which matched what she was feeling between her legs. Sitting up and pulling up her knees, Rock offered her his hand to help her to her feet. Reluctantly she took it and stood before him. Smirking, Rock walked away as Jenna turned to see Scotty arguing wildly with the director over the shot. The two men who had been friends and former roommates since they came to California over ten years ago now were coming to an agreement on something she could not discern. Jenna stepped off stage as Missy came in for her close up shots of the scene. Taking a spot behind the sound guy, Jenna watched the girl flub her lines over, and over, not hitting her mark once.

"Jen!" Scotty called to her.

"Yes?"

"Take these to Rock's trailer." Scotty handed her a prop semi-automatic nine-millimeter and the next day's schedule. Without hesitation, Jenna took them and headed towards Rock's trailer. Holding the weapon with the easy grace of a seasoned gunman, Scotty watched and admired her comfortable ability with the firearm. Since the day, she started stunt school Jenna took to the guns with a natural ease and was a damn good shot. Many times over the last year, they drove to the high desert and busted off rounds like banditos, shooting cans and any other targets they could find. Walking cautiously in spike heels across the loose earth, Jenna thought of one time she out-shot Scotty, an expert sharpshooter. Maybe he let her win, she decided.

At the trailer door, Jenna breathed deeply to steady herself, keep her composure and she tried not to think of how much Rock heated her insides as he pinned his body against her. Even now, she felt an aching between her legs for him.

Banging loudly got no response, and she waited, looking behind her for Scotty. Without looking, she reached up to knock again and put her tiny hand directly on Rock's privates. Dripping wet in nothing but a towel, he stood with his hands on his hips, looking down where she touched him. But Jenna was lost in the amazement of his wet muscles and what lie beneath the towel. She licked her lips until he cleared his throat and Jenna jerked her hand away quickly. She lifted up the gun and schedule to him.

"Sorry. These are for you." Jenna lowered her eyes in extreme embarrassment.

After swiping the items from her, he slammed the door in her face.

"You're welcome," Jenna whispered as she walked away.

After meeting back up with Tracy, the two girls went to the Chinatown set, where the frantic director cursed wildly and slammed a scrip on his knees.

"Where the hell is Missy?" he demanded loudly.

"She's locked herself in her trailer, again." Tracy shrugged. The director picked up his script and pointed it at Jenna. "Son of a bitch. Hey, you."

"Me?" Jenna pointed to her herself.

"Stand here and say this line."

He left her no choice and pushed the script at her. Jenna read it, memorized it quickly, and handed it the papers back to her friend. Jenna delivered the line perfectly in one take.

"Cut, print. Thanks everyone, good job, Jan." The director relaxed in his chair.

"Oh thanks but it's Jen." Surprised at the recognition, Jenna grinned and turned to walk off the set. She didn't see Rock watching her from afar.

"Come on I want to show you my shoes," Tracy said pulling on her arm.

"Sure, let me check in with Scotty, I'll be right there."

Rock stood back in a shadow, studying her smile as she tucked hair behind her ear and greeted other extras. Observing her until she disappeared from his sight, Rock shook his head trying to clear her from his thoughts and went back to work.

Finding Scotty going over schedules in his trailer, Jenna inquired about the next shot. "What time will you need me back?"

"Six-thirty, come back here then," Scotty told her without looking away from the papers. She bounced away, rushing to Tracy's tent. Many of the actors and extras usually camped out on the location to save time, energy and gas money, and she happened to be one of them.

"Check these puppies out!" Tracy held up the funky platform heels.

Jenna took the shoes out of the box to examine them. "Cool."

"They're CMF's!" Tracy told her excitedly.

"What does that mean?" Jenna asked greenly.

"Come fuck me's. Hopefully, if I play my cards right tonight …"

"Eric's back from Seattle?" Jenna asked about her boyfriend.

"No," Tracy purred.

"Then who? What a minute. Jared? You're sleeping with Jared?"

"Well, we haven't yet but tonight could be it. Don't say anything to anyone; you know how fast rumors and gossip fly around here. Like you and Scotty."

"What? Scotty and I are just friends. We never!" Jenna told her innocently.

"And then there's what happened with Rock earlier." Tracy prodded.

"You heard about that? I didn't mean to touch his dick."

Tracey raised an eyebrow. "No, I was referring to you two going after each other like arch enemies or shit."

Jenna's face flushed. "Oh my god, when he pinned me down I thought I was going to have an orgasm right then and there. He felt huge!"

"Maybe you should borrow these for tonight." Tracey dangled the shoes.

"Maybe." Jenna bit her lip. Jenna thought back to the first day to stunt school. She really thought Rock would be there, but instead she found Scotty. Scotty first words to her echoed in her mind. You have potential I could see it as soon as you opened that door. He taught her everything she knew and did it all with a patience of a monk.

They trained for weeks, and on one particular night, Scotty noticed her lack of energy.

"What's going on here, why I can't get you to do this?" he asked about on certain move.

"I'll get it, let me try again." Jenna tried again but failed almost collapsing onto the floor mat.

"Jenna, tell me what's going on," he asked in a stern voice. Jenna stared and gave in, she knew she could trust Scotty more than anyone in the world.

"I haven't eaten anything."

"Well eat something," He said.

"In days," she said softly.

"What? Why not?"

"I don't have any money. I had to pay my tuition … and I have been living in my car."

"You are going to stay with me," he said.

"No, Scotty I could not do that."

"You can and you will, I can not have my star pupil off her game. Come let's go get some dinner." He said putting her in a headlock and rubbing his knuckles over her hair playfully.

"I owe ya," she said as he released her.

"You are my friend, that's payment enough." He replied.

The shoot went late into the night and way over schedule. Jenna was exhausted, hot, tired, and just wanted to lie down and sleep. Her body was trained for physical activity but now it had reached a painful limit. When she was finally, mercifully released from the set Scotty walked Jenna through the darkened set back to her tent. Twinkling stars that danced wildly peppered the easing darkness in the early morning sky. Jenna looked up at them, wondering if Rock was looking at them as well.

"Do you need anything before I go?" Scotty asked.

"No, thanks for walking me back … Wait—there is one thing."

"What's that?" he said, smiling.

Jenna wiped a smudge from his cheek. "How did I do today?"

"You made me proud; keep it up. Be at wardrobe at 9:30 sharp." He scratched his nose and turned away.

"Will do," she said as she watched him walk away into the early morning desert light.

In her tent, she undressed, peeling off the cat suit, which was no easy task. It stuck to her skin like tape, pulling her flesh tight and making a sucking sound as she jerked it off.

"Gross, I stink. I have to shower," she said to no one. Wrapping a towel around her, she padded lightly to the mobile showers to wash away the day. Steam poured out of the curtain as she lathered her hair and rinsed the conditioner from it. Closing her eyes and leaning her head back, she let the water run down her back soothing her sore muscles. Jenna was nearly falling asleep standing up.

The creaking of the door jolted her awake. Not hearing another shower running, she called out nervously.

"Is someone out there? Hello?" Turning off the water, she wrapped a towel around her body and walked out of the shower into the locker room.

"Anyone there?"

No response. A slight shiver crept down her spine as another low noise caught her ear. Grabbing her tank top and shorts, Jenna nearly dove into the clothes, slipped into her flip-flops, and hurried toward the door.

"Whoa!" She yelled as her feet slipped in the liquid that stained the floor, and her head smacked into the locker handle as she fell to the floor with a loud thud. Conditioner had squirted all over the floor and covered her flip-flops.

"O-oh." Jenna grunted as she felt her head. The liquid that trickled from her temple above her eye in her hairline wasn't shampoo. Getting up, Jenna felt dizzy and she stumbled to the sink to rinse the goo off her shoes. Holding her towel to her head she tried clean off the blood the best could in a hurry. She wanted out of there fast. Someone was in there and she wanted out.

The clock read one fifty-nine a.m. as Jenna stepped back into her tent. But Jenna felt unsafe, too shook up to be alone; so she fled to Scotty's trailer. Noticing his light was still on, she crept out into the darkness and knocked softly on the trailer door.

His door flew open. "What are you doing here?"

"Can I come in?" She was shaking from the cool night air and her still-wet hair. Standing in nothing but a pair of boxers, Scotty opened the door to let her pass.

"Did I wake you?" she asked.

He stared at her curiously. "No, I was going over tomorrow's rundown. What happened to your head?"

"I, um, fell." She hoped he believed her.

"Come on, Jen, there's more to it." He looked at her patiently.

"I was in the shower and I heard someone come in. I called out, but no one answered then I didn't hear anything else. I was a little freaked out, so I got dressed, but I slipped on conditioner. It was squirted all over the floor like on purpose! I smacked my head on the handle on the lockers when I fell down."

"Are you okay?" he asked, pushing back her hair.

She wasn't. "Can I crash on your couch?"

He shook his head and stepped aside. "You can have the bed."

"No, I can't put you out of your own bed." Jenna hesitated.

"Come on." He put his arm around her shoulder and led her to the tiny bedroom. Covered with masculine gray and black designer sheets, the full-size bed took up the entire room.

"Thanks Scotty. You're the best."

"I know, go to sleep." He hit her on the rump with a script as she crawled over the sheets. She was asleep before her head hit the pillow.

Scotty stood for a few minutes in the doorway and watched her sleeping like an angel. Walking to Jenna, he pulled up the covers over his friend, sat next to her on the bed and brushed aside her hair to get a better look at the cut in her hairline. *God, she is so sweet,* he thought, leaning over, kissing her lightly on the forehead. He sighed, stood up and walked out the dark bedroom, closed the door, and went back to his work.

The sun pierced through the window. Jenna's eyes saw blinding white as she awoke the next morning.

"Shit, I overslept! What time is it?" Jenna jumped up but pain made her hold her head. She felt like she had a hangover and reached blindly for the alarm clock. It read nine a.m.

"Oh, good." Her heart beat hard as she fell back on the bed and tried to calm down.

In nothing but her tank top and shorts, Jenna shivered as the cold morning air chilled her. Her erect nipples showed clearly through the thin fabric of her shirt. I can't walk out like this, she thought and threw on one of Scotty's button-up shirts. He was already gone. I'd better get to wardrobe and make up early for once, she thought.

Opening the door, her sunshine-blinded eyes focused on the men standing outside Scotty's trailer. Mortified that Scotty, Rock, Jared, his brother and four other various crew members spotted her walking out of Scotty's trailer wearing what appeared to be nothing but his shirt, Jenna high-tailed it to the wardrobe tent, reeling with humiliation.

"Oh great, now Rock thinks I am screwing Scotty," Jenna complained to Tracy who was in the make up chair next to her. "Ugh, why do I always make an ass out of myself?"

"Shit happens. Damn, look at your head. Did that happen on set last night?"

Jenna felt her head. "Yeah, it um happened last night." Not wanting to go into the details, Jenna changed the subject as the make artist entered into the room.

"What do you have going for the next scene?" Tracy asked.

She nodded at the cosmetic professional. "I have the fight scene at the top of the building and onto the window-washing scaffold. How about you?"

"Waitress number two," Tracy said.

"How exciting!" Jenna teased sarcastically.

On the set, Jenna noticed it was buzzing with people who were setting up equipment, and scrambling to get everything in place. Jenna's heart flip-flopped as Rock stood next to Scotty. She was not sure if she was excited or still embarrassed from Rock watching her leave the trailer. Deciding to leave it at a mild mix of both, Jenna walked onto the set and looked around.

"Jen, I need you over here." Scotty briefed her and Rock on exactly how many swings and punches he wanted. He practiced with them for a half-hour and then let Rock and Jenna work it out between themselves.

Rock leaned into Jen. "I need the slap to look as realistic as possible, so when I get my hand to the out side of your shoulder start you head turn. Clear?"

"Yes. Like this?" She showed Rock the move.

"Good. Let's try that." In a few practice runs, they had it down perfectly.

Man, he is such a great stunt man, his timing so perfect and thorough. Jenna marveled as she observed his technique and form.

"Okay, I need Rock and Jessica to the lift," the assistant director called out.

"Um, it is Jenna, not Jessica," she said through grinned teeth. As she stepped onto the window-washing lift, her stomach pitched its liquid up into her throat.

She looked over the rail. Her sparing partner adjusting his safety lines, and he caught a glance of her face turning pale as the ground grew distant from them. Rock noticed her holding onto the railing with a white-knuckled death grip.

"Why didn't they shoot this on a green screen set?" she grumbled to herself.

He answered with out looking at her. "Too expensive."

"Oh," she responded blankly. Rock looked up as they reached the roof. Swinging over the rail, he surveyed the area and then helped her over the ledge. Once again, she checked her equipment.

"Ready?" he asked her. Nodding together in agreement, they took their positions and gave the thumbs-up to crew on the ground. Having radio contact through earpieces, Jenna, Scotty, and Rock were all linked on the same frequency. With his finger to his earpiece, Rock spoke. "It's a go."

"Action," Scotty replied.

The two went through the motions of each precise hit and kick until it came to the dramatic slap. Blown off balance a few centimeters by a slight and sudden wind, Jenna's small frame wobbled mere inches, right into the path of

Rock's large hard hand. Knocked to her knees, Jenna gasped but he spoke quickly, "Keep it going."

"Ahhgghh." She growled as she jumped up and swung her leg at him, sending him flying to back to the scaffolding as planned. What came next shocked the hell out of the both of them. As he landed on the suspended platform, his safety cable snapped like a cracked whip. Rock staggered a few steps backwards, sending him back too far and nearly over the railing,

"Rock!" Jenna yelled.

"Scotty! His harness broke!" She shouted into her earpiece.

Steadied for the moment, Rock put a hand up to signal he was okay. Jenna exhaled a deep breathe of relief which was quickly recoiled.

Crack! Like a shot of thunder, the platform's cables gave way on one side sending Rock's body speeding down the vertical metal slide.

"Shit!" he yelled as he slid twenty feet to the edge.

Gasping, Jenna could only watch as he slid to the edge and over it. Only one hand kept Rock clinging to the half-inch lip at the end. Without hesitating, Jenna ran to the broken platform and jumped to his side. Scotty screamed in their earpieces.

"Don't do it!"

Before Scotty got words out, she was in the air and landing on her ass sliding down to Rock, whose fingers tips were barely holding on. A sharp jerk from the safety wire stopped her five feet from reaching him.

"Are you crazy!" Scotty buzzed in her earpiece.

The only way I can reach him is if I take off this harness, she reasoned. Bracing her legs against one of the side poles, she pushed up enough to get some slack to undo the safety wire.

"What the hell are you doing?" Rock yelled up at her.

In her ear, Scotty screamed. "Do not unhook yourself!"

Yanking the earpiece out, she unhooked the link and slid on her belly further to the end. Hooking her legs around a side rail, Jenna grabbed Rock's wrist and with all her strength tried to pull him up. The scaffolding shifted and swayed in the wind. Rock struggled to hold on with two hands but lost his grip on the first one. Looking down to the ground fifty or so feet below he let out another curse until he heard Jenna calling to him.

"Take my hand!" Jenna reached for him. Rock looked up and clung to her, their eyes meeting, silently pleading with each other not to let go. Rock took a trusting chance and swung his free hand up. In that very moment as they locked wrists, their hearts locked together as well, sealing the bond of trust between them. Tugging with all her strength, she struggled to keep her legs hold on as tight, keeping enough of a grip on him that he could use her body to pull himself up enough to get one of his hands on the railing. Rock held tight to her wrist as he tried to get his entire body up to the railing but stopped as he heard the earsplitting scream she let out. The muscles in her legs tore as the weight of him wrenched down as the swaying, broken platform lowered slowly down to the ground. Fighting through the pain, Jenna held on with every once of strength she had left, not giving up on her grip on him for a second.

"Ten more feet." Rock told her. Unable to see her face, Rock could feel her body shaking and knew she was in tremendous pain. The agony was too much to bear and Jenna legs gave out just they made it to the ground. Rock stopped her from falling onto the dirt as everyone rushed in to survey both of their conditions.

"I'm okay," he said as the crew rushed to his aid. Pushing aside them all, Scotty raced to give Jenna a sharp tongue-lashing, but changed his mind as Rock held him back. He could see her lying on her stomach moaning in pain. Rock let go of him and Scotty fell to his knees.

"Where are you hurt?" Scotty asked.

Jenna wheezed, "My legs ... pulled muscles." She could barely get the words out as she lay face down on the ground. Later Scotty would yell at her for taking such a damn risk, but right now, he wanted to take her to the first aid tent.

"Can you walk?" he asked as he put his hand on her shoulder. She tried to turn over but the pain made Jenna cry out like a wounded animal. Everyone in earshot cringed in sympathy as she bit her lip to keep from howling in agony. Scooping her up into his arms, Scotty held her as Rock approached him.

"Give her to me. You need to go check that out." Rock nodded at the stunt helper who held deliberately cut wires. Tears of pain streamed down her face as he placed his arm behind her back and gently under her tender knees and carried her in his long, strong arms. Placing her face against Rock's chest, she listened to his heart beating a frenzied pace. As he carried her the hundred yards across to the first aid tent, she did not say a word but simply shook her head when he asked if his grip was too tight. Placing her down as cautiously as he could muster, Rock watched her pretty face wince as the doctor asked her to roll over on her stomach.

"Well what do we have?" the studio doctor inquired.

"Hamstrings pulled, can't stand up," Jenna squeaked out.

The doctor said as he pulled on exam gloves, "Let's check it out."

An unbelievable wail came from deep in her throat as he placed his trained hands over the legs and butt muscles and applied pressure. Rock let her squeeze his hand as she cried out. Whew, he thought. She got some grip for such a tiny thing.

After finishing his exam, the doctor told her, "You'll have to be off the legs for a few days to a week. Maybe more."

"No, I can't, I have to finish the shoot."

"Ice and heat, alternate every fifteen minutes now and then one time every hour. In a day or two try to flex the muscles. Do you have someone that can take care of you for a few days?"

Jenna shook her head. She had no one. Rock took notice.

"Take these crutches; they will help keep pressure off the muscles."

"Thank you, Doc," Jenna said.

"No working for a week!" he reminded her as his assistant gave her ice packs, and sent her on her way. Rock was not about to let her walk. Picking her up effortlessly, he took her from the tent and straight to his trailer.

"My tent is that way." She pointed the opposite direction. He did not look at her or respond but kept walking until they were in his trailer, and he moved carefully, trying not to bang her legs in the door way. Placing her into his bed, he waited while she rolled over slowly and it was a few minutes until the pain subsided from the movement.

"You don't have to do this; I'll be fine in my tent."

"You saved my life. It's the least I can do. But you should have listened to Scotty; you could have killed yourself." He leaned in the doorway.

I'd do it all over again, she thought.

"I thought you were a goner," she said as he stepped closer and crouched down next to her, placing the ice pack on her legs.

"Thank you." she said, but what she thought was kiss me, kiss me now you hot hunk of a man. As he leaned over her, looking closely at her face, he reached out and brushed a silky lock of hair from her forehead. She could feel the heat from his breath over her mouth. She licked her lips and closed her eyes, wishing for his mouth to ravish hers. A loud banging on the door interrupted what might have been a classic Hollywood kissing scene.

"Rock, it's Scotty. Do you have Jenna in there?"

Opening her eyes, she saw Rock's broad back as he approached the door.

"Hey man, come on in." Rock opened the door.

"You okay?" Scotty asked.

"Fine, but Jenna is out for a week."

"What's the diagnosis?"

"Pulled hamstrings both legs."

Scotty sighed. "That was pretty damn stupid what she did."

"I can hear you." Jenna chimed in.

Walking into the bedroom, Scotty he threw up his arms. "What the hell were you thinking?"

"Scotty, he would have fallen, there was no time to think, I just reacted. Wouldn't you have done the same?" She shrugged, giving him her best grin.

"When I tell you to do something, you need to listen!" Scotty retorted sharply.

"Don't be too hard on her Scotty, right or wrong, she saved my life." Rock said, and the other man seemed to calm.

"What did you find out?" Rock asked, changing the subject.

"Well the cables were deliberately cut, along with your harness."

"What!" Jenna shouted and turned, causing more pain. "Damn, that hurts!"

"I checked all the equipment myself a half hour before we started," Rock stated.

Jenna was mystified. "Who the hell would want to hurt Rock?"

"I would like to know." Rock agreed.

Scotty checked his watch. "We have to keep this quiet; we're calling an emergency meeting with Jared in ten minutes."

"But I can't walk," Jenna pouted.

The two men looked at each other, exasperated.

Rock went to his mini fridge, took out bottle of water, and gave her two painkillers and ordered her to take them. "Trust me, okay?"

So infatuated with the kindness he was showing, she simply nodded obediently. He handed Jenna the remote to the flat screen mounted on the wall. "Relax. We'll be back in a while."

Watching as the two men stepped out of the trailer; she opened the water and took the pills he gave to her. Jenna jumped as she heard the door being locked from the outside. Suddenly washing over her was her worst fear, feeling alone.

For over a year, she had wanted this moment, to be in Rock's bed, but getting laid, not laid up. The ice packs sweated over the back of her legs and dripped beads of cold water between her legs giving her a quick jolt of pleasure. Gingerly, gently she turned, desperately trying not to move the hamstrings, but it hurt like hell. When are these pills going to kick in? Switching on the television to the entertainment channel, Jenna was surprised by a news bulletin and paid close attention.

"Shocking new video of a death-defying rescue on Missy Manga's new movie." A flashy reporter stared at the camera in concern.

"What!" Jenna yelled at the television. The ten-second clip showed her jumping on the broken platform that Rock hung from, unhooking her harness. Then the picture went right to a shot of Missy's face.

"You've got to be kidding me! They made her look like she saved Rock!"

Jenna switched off the set as she settled into the soft, comfortable mattress. The pain from her legs subsided, the drugs kicked in, and she fell into a foggy sleep. For hours, she dreamed horrible nightmares of being unable to get to Rock, him slipping out of her hands over and over in a loop of bad horror movies. Her restless body thrashed around the bed and she woke in a sudden panic-laden cold sweat. For a minute, she forgot where she was. Looking around the dark room she found her bearings and remembered she was sleeping in Rock Constantine's bed. The alarm clock read two twenty-two a.m.

Another, different pain bedeviled her. "I have to pee. Damn, how in the world am I going to pull this off?" Moving to the edge of the bed, she stood lightly on the less sore of her two legs and crept like a sloth the ten steps to the bathroom. Relieving herself, she washed her face and ran some toothpaste over her teeth with her finger. Quickly taking a sniff of Rock's Farhenheight cologne, she set it down and turned off the light. As she opened the door, Jenna ran smack into Rock's naked massive chest, scaring her enough to let out a yelp.

"What are you doing?" he asked her sternly.

"I, um had to you know, go."

"You shouldn't be walking, I would have carried you."

"I didn't know if you were here, besides they feel a little better."

He looked down at her, and she looked at the couch that still held his body's imprint and then back at him—wearing nothing but a pair of plaid boxer shorts.

"You don't have to sleep on the couch, I'm sure it's not as comfortable your own bed. I mean were both adults. We can sleep together, I mean lay down next to each other." Jenna stumbled over her tongue.

He picked her up in an effortless, sweeping motion. Placing his arms under her legs and behind her back, he took her back to the bed, and placed her on the cool sheets. A moment later, he crawled in next to her and propped his body on his arm. Jenna's heart raced and the blood rushed between her legs. A panicked excitement filled her being. Looking into her eyes, he told her to roll-over to her stomach.

"What?"

"Trust me." His manner left no choice.

"Okay." Nervous excitement made her forget the pain as she turned over slowly. Rock's low voice sounded like heaven as he spoke, "This may hurt at first."

In her mind Jenna said, "Make it hurt daddy, give it to me to me good."

He put his hot hands over her shoulders, rubbing them roughly in a circular motion. Moving his fingers down her spine, he traced along every inch, stretching her back muscles. Pressure on her tailbone made her push her hips into the mattress and shot her libido into overdrive. Moaning in pleasure, she caught herself and stopped, hoping he would not read too much into it. As he made his way across her small firm ass, he rubbed it and all her muscles tightened in shock.

"Relax," he commanded.

She tried as best she could as his brawny hands came dangerously close her swelling womanhood. She could not hold back the guttural moan as his fingers lined the crease where her thigh and butt met. She let a low moan slip out, as eyes closed tightly and winced. Kneading and stretching the flesh on the back of her thigh, it helped loosen the sore muscle as the heat from his hands sent shock waves pulsating between her legs.

"Oh Rock. Oh it feels so good." She moaned.

He moved back to up slowly to her butt and lower back, sliding his hands up the sides of her chest. Am I imagining this or did he just brush the sides of my breasts?

She could not take the torture any more. Rolling over, Jenna put her hands around his neck and pulled his face to hers. She kissed him with a passion that took him completely by surprise. Holding his face in her hands, Jenna gave it all. She had nothing to lose. Jenna never felt this way about man. From the first moment she saw this gorgeous man on screen, she felt like she had been struck by a lightning bolt of love. He reminded her so much of her father. Tall, dark, strong like him but her father did not want her. He left her broken and bruised; mentality and physically abandoned in a homeless shelter at the age of nine. Jenna would have done anything to make her daddy happy so he would stay. The last words he spoke to her stung in her mind, "If you really want something, go after it, no matter what the consequences." Her father seemed to believe so much in this, he left her sleeping to wake up all alone. Now she took his advice. She wanted Rock. Wanted to be wanted by Rock. She wanted to be loved, no matter what the consequences.

Rock's surprise registered brightly on his face. Where is this coming from? He thought as she pulled his face to hers. She is aggressive he contemplated. He could sense that desperation in her lips. The fearless gusto she showed gave him a kick. He liked her spunk and tenacity and the fact she risked her life to save him. Something the pop tart would not even consider. Nevertheless, what he really liked were the soft wanting lips and tight body lying under his. Not one to let his guard down, he paused. The random sex and women only fulfilled was old the desire of his libido, but Jenna crept pass that barrier of physical skin. Her essence started to pulse through his veins, pumping from nerves to brain to sex and back to rest in his heart. Opening his eyes, he caught hers, that brown green so familiar, so haunting. He strained to place them in the index up his mind. Eyes that were kind, loving, forgiving and mothering. Then it struck him. The color the same perfectly blended shade of greens and browns were that of his mother. The last time he had seen his mother's eyes were when they stared up at him as he found her body dead after leaping from her death at the family estate in Romania. Jenna survived her leap unlike his beloved mother. The anger rose at the memory. He had to push it from his mind. Rid it from his thoughts. He needed a release, one that would free the emotional torment. Jenna was there, kissing him, begging him to respond, so he did, finding his release.

At first, he did not respond to her kiss, but as she moaned and licked his lips, he parted his mouth and ravished her mouth by sliding his tongue into hers. He explored her mouth with his while his hands did the same with her tiny body. He moved away from her mouth, burying his face into her neck and moved down to her chest. He tried, oh how he tried to stay away, to think rationally but since the first day he saw her on set, he had a lusted for her and now he allowed himself the pleasure of letting his feelings go rampant.

"Oh, Rock I have wanted you for so long." Jenna ran her hands down his back, dragging her nails up the length till she tangled her fingers in his long, silky hair, which drove him nuts.

"Jenna, stop, your legs," he warned.

"I don't care about the pain, I want you so bad."

As they indulged each other's mouths wildly, she rolled over on top of his chest, Jenna screamed as the Charley horses cramped both legs.

"Oh Rock, oh Charley!"

"Jenna, you make me so hard … what? Did you just call me Charley?"

"No, Charley horses in both legs, oh it hurts so bad, oh god," she cried out thunderously. Tears spilled out as the knots contracted so tightly, paralyzing her in pain. Sitting up, Rock quickly worked on the muscles, applying pressure to specific points and dissipating the knots after a few minutes. Rock felt her reaction through every touch of his strong hands. He knew how painful the cramps could be, having them once or twice from creature suits he had for various movies. Placing his warm, tight hands over the back of her thighs, he worked the tendons and ligaments repeatedly. He made his way down her legs to her feet and back up her calves and thighs and on to her ass. She felt like Jell-O.

Jenna purred with pleasure. "You made them go away. Thank you."

"You're welcome," he said as he brushed her blonde hair aside with one hand, and rubbed the back of her neck with the other. This is my fantasy come true, she sighed and fell asleep as he rubbed and massaged her knotting muscles back to normal.

Rock, sexually frustrated, could only sigh, but he was glad she was not in pain. Besides he could wait; she may just be worth it.

As the sun lighted the room, Jenna rubbed her eyes open and glanced around for a sign of her sexy savior.

"Damn, I hate to wake up alone," Jenna said, finding the empty space where he had lain. Standing on wobbly legs, she grabbed crutches and headed out the trailer door. She made sure there was no audience this time.

"Cool, no one around. I am so freaking hungry."

Still in her sleep shorts and tank top, Jenna opened the door, trying to maneuver down the steps. Sharp cramps jolted into her hamstrings and sent her tumbling down face first in the dusty dirt with a profound thud.

"What the hell are you doing out of bed?" Scotty barked at her.

"I was hungry," he said sheepishly, grimacing as he picked her up.

Taking her back into the trailer, he scolded her like child. "Why can't you follow doctor's order?"

She shrugged. "Have you found out anything?"

"No," Scotty said.

"Did you see the news last night?" she asked him.

He frowned. "What, you talked to the news?"

"No ... someone on set shot the rescue on home movie camera and they splashed it all over the entertainment showcase."

"Who shot it?" Scotty asked.

Jenna slipped the crutches under her arms. "They didn't say."

"Here." Scotty handed her the duffle bag and purse from her tent. "I'll have Tracy bring you something to eat. Stay off your legs. Please."

"Yes sir," she teased, saluting him. "You *will* let me know when you find out who did this."

"Yes. Stay off the legs!" he ordered before shutting the trailer door.

Jenna sniffed under her arms and decided to go against Scotty's orders and at least take a shower before getting off her feet. Undressing and stepping into the trailer shower, she braced her body against the wall as she lathered up with the apple shampoo, and fruity shower gel she used to shave. Done, clean and shaven in twenty minutes, she sat the on the lid of the toilet naked to rub scented lotions over shapely legs and toned arms.

The bathroom door swung open. Rock stood staring at her perfect five-foot buff body for a very long moment before slamming the door shut. "Sorry."

Jenna smiled as she looked into the mirror.

For just this situation, Jenna kept a set of sexy underwear in her bag. She covered the sheer fabric of her lingerie with a tank top and terry-cloth mini skirt. Emerging from the steamed up bathroom, she found Rock in his trailer making up the bed.

In unison, they both blurted out, "about last night." He stood, his expression pained. Foolishness washed over her and she regretted putting on the sexy underwear. As she tried to maneuver around him to leave, her crutch stuck on the bed rail and she clumsily attempted to free it.

"Where are you going?" he asked as he watched her trying to untangle the crutch.

"I feel like I have overstayed my welcome," Jenna smiled ruefully.

Putting his hands on her smoothed scented shoulders, he rubbed his strong hands down her arms and back up, feeling the firm muscles of her upper arms.

"I want you to stay," Rock said.

"You do?"

He leaned over and kissed her gently on her soft full lips. Her eyelids fluttered as he pulled away.

"I—I could stay for a while." Jenna sat on the bed. He turned his back to her, walked to the front of the trailer, locked the door, and closed the shades. *Oh boy, it's on now,* she told herself.

Coming back, standing in front of her, he took off his shirt to reveal the hard, toned, ripped body. Jenna swallowed hard as he took off her flip-flops and rubbed her feet. A thousand nerve endings bolted through her system as he ran his hands up her calves and knees. Between her legs ached and burned, as he crawled up the bed and over her. Breasts perky at full attention caught his eye as he scanned his deep brown eyes over her body. Her nipples went so hard that the sheer fabric burned as it rubbed over them. He engaged her lips with his as he plunged his tongue into her mouth, sucking and kissing in frenzy. Stopping and rearing up he yanked her top off with lightening speed. Staring and panting like a savage at her fully erect nipples, he capped his mouth over the fabric teasing them with his tongue and teeth. Frantically, he worked on the back clasp of her bra trying to free her breasts so he could feel the naked flesh in his hot mouth. Popping the bra off after several attempts, he drove his mouth over the right nipple and massaged the left his hand, as her breasts swelled from the excitement. Reaching around his toned chest, she ran her hands down his back feeling every solid rippling muscles through his smooth, hot skin. He's so damn gorgeous, raced through her mind. So much so, it made her tingle with nervous energy. Pressing his flesh over her naked chest sent bolts of electric pulses racing across every nerve ending. Kissing her mouth again, his hands ran roughly over the sides of her chest down to her hips. Instinctively she dug her nails into his back, dragging them downward sending him into full erection mode. His dick was large, thick, and pulsating as it pressed between her thighs. Jenna gasped as she felt it sticking her though the fabric of her skirt. Rearing up, Rock pulled back, pulling her skirt down in one rough yank, sending the panties off with it. Lying there, he positioned his head in between her legs. Nearly crushing his skull between her thighs as he drove his hot mouth into folds, he took his arms, one on each leg her pull her legs open wider carefully, as he sucked and licked her hot, pink snatch. Building pressure sent her into unearthly ecstasy and she begged him to suck harder.

"Don't stop, I'm can't hold it any longer. I'm going to come …" Before she could finish her sentence, the tidal wave crashed as the orgasm felt like a damn bursting its walls repeatedly, her first true orgasm.

"Rock, I want you in me, I need you in me."

He reached over to the nightstand, pulling open a small drawer and producing a condom. Ripping the package open with his teeth, he threw the package who knows where, as he tried to fit the rubber over his huge, straight member. As soon as it was in place, he fell onto her and drove directly into to her hot wet opening. The pain from her injury was non-existent as all she felt was his solid shaft pushed deeper and deeper into her. Hearing her crying out in sheer pleasure, he could barely keep his load from shooting out every time he heard her squealing in pleasure.

"Unfuckingbelievable!" was all he could think, as she tightened her inner muscles around his cock while inside her slick tunnel. One thrust went so deep; she jumped up and knocked her skull to his.

"Sorry," she panted. "I want you to call my name when you come," she begged as he hammered into her for what seemed like forever. He growled like a beast as she sucked his neck and moved on to stick her tongue in his ear. It was too much for him to hold back, he shouted as the liquid burst out like a cannon from his balls down his huge shaft.

"Oh Jenna, Agggh. Here it comes, Jenna!" His face turned Japanese from the mind-altering orgasm flooding into the end of the condom. Collapsing on top her, they drowned in each other sweat and heat. She smothered his neck and face with kisses as her legs shook from the intensity of the sex session.

"You okay?" he asked.

"Uh-huh." She said, panting heavily. He rolled off her and went into the bathroom to take care of the condom. Jenna rolled over as she heard the sound of the shower and she quickly fell asleep.

Exiting the shower in only a towel, Rock stood over her watching the muscles on the back of her legs and butt twitching. He wanted to wake her up and do it again, but the sight of her sleeping so sweetly, he resisted.

Crawling into the bed next to her little hot body, he watched her sleeping so soundly. Thinking about her, he was mixed up; this girl he's known for a few days, he's made love to her already. He felt like knew her forever. Sure, he had plenty of fucks in his life but something was different She made him feel—he was not quite sure what or why, but she did. Deciding to let her sleep, Rock went off to catch up with Scotty in the training tent.

Two hours later, Rock went back to the trailer to find Jenna awake and sitting up, brushing her long blonde hair. Looking up as he entered the trailer, he found her in his t-shirt smiling widely as he repeated the expression. He leaned down and kissed her head.

"Hungry?"

"Starving. But first …" She pulled him down to her and they went at it like rabbits again.

He helped her dress and took her out of the trailer to mess hall. Gentleman that he was, Rock carried her tray over to the table. She thanked him graciously as he set her crutches to the side.

Leaving her with Tracy, he strolled off to work on some set-ups with rest of the stunt crew.

"I'm done with all my scenes," Tracy told her.

"Really? Are you going to leave?" Jenna asked her friend.

"For a few days. I'm going back to L.A. to catch up on bills, laundry, and clean my apartment. What are you going to do?"

Jenna thought for a moment. "I have no idea; I haven't seen Scotty all day."

"I heard you saw plenty of Rock," Tracy said coyly.

She frowned. "What exactly are you implying?"

"You've been in his trailer for like a day. Wait a minute! You screwed him."

"Shhh, keep your voice down," Jenna said quickly.

"Spill the details, now or I will yell it out, you slut."

Laughing the two girls huddled together. "Best lay ever. He is so amazing in bed."

"And …?"

"Hee-huge!"

"Shut the hell up. Did he go down?"

"Oh yeah, my first. I mean best orgasm, ever!"

"So, you going to stay on set with him?"

"Actually I wouldn't mind going back to my apartment and getting fresh clothes and stuff but I can't drive my VW, it's a stick and there's no way I could push in the clutch. Where do you live?" Jenna asked.

Tracy drew on the table with her finger. "Right at Franklin and Highland. In the old Hollywood Art School."

"Shut up, I live on North Orchid just west of Franklin. We are, like in walking distance of each other." Jenna laughed.

"My roommate just moved out, I need a new one. Move in with me. I have two bedrooms with a small private courtyard."

Jenna considered this. "Well, my lease is up next month."

"Maybe Rock will ask you to move in," Tracy teased.

"It's way too soon, but I do know where he lives. I Googled him when I found out I got the job." Jenna leaned closer to her friend. "He lives in the Hollywood Hills."

"Stalker."

They laughed and parted ways.

Swinging across the set on her crutches, Jenna made her way over to Scotty's trailer. Banging on the door with the end of the crutch, she got no response.

"Where is every one?" she wondered. The set seemed deserted as she moved across it. Being around so many people on set comforted her. However, with the eerie calm and quiet Jenna felt uneasy. She thought of Rock. He made her so happy, finally having him desire her. She waited so long to for this; the months she put into stunt school, every moment was for this time in her life. She hoped he would be done with his scenes early so she could touch him, taste him, and kiss him again. Maybe he is done; she thought and headed over to find out.

Back at his trailer, after a long, hard day working on a fast-paced motorcycle chase scene, Rock showered and crawled exhausted and naked into bed. He left the door unlocked hoping Jenna would come back and lay her hot, short body next to him for a repeat performance. Drifting quickly into a deep sleep, he did not notice that she had done exactly as he wished until she was in his arms. Topless, she snuggled up next to him. Half asleep, he rolled over on top of her and kissed her. She smelled different, tasted different, felt different. She pulled him close, covered her mouth to his, just as the overhead flicked on. There, in the doorway, standing motionless, mouth wide open, was Jenna. She stumbled back, bumping into the door jam as she fumbled her way out. Rock looked at her in confusion and tried to processing what was going on. Missy lay under him laughing wildly.

"What the hell are you doing in here?" he barked at her.

She smiled wickedly. "I knew when you looked at me on the set today; you wanted to fuck me tonight."

"Are you out of your mind?" Rock stammered.

"Oops, did I make your girl jealous? Oh, my mistake," the actress said coolly as she rose, picked up her shirt, and walked out of the trailer, leaving Rock feeling as if he was in the twilight zone.

Dragging her duffle bag and purse behind her as she swung the crutches across the dirt, Jenna made her way to the parking lot at the edge of the studio's property. Throwing the bags in the backseat of her Volkswagen, she wrestled with the crutches trying to fit them in between the seats. Before she could get to the driver's seat, Rock jerked her back by the arm.

"Where do you think you're going?" he asked.

"What do you care …" she sniffled, trying to hold back tears. She wrenched her arm away.

"Let me explain, it's not what you think …"

"Oh, I understand completely, I was just another notch on your black belt, I guess I was wrong to think that maybe you really liked me. That we had a bit of chemistry. My mistake you … you … man whore!"

Getting in the car, she slammed the door. She was not going anywhere; her keys were still in the door.

"Damn it!" she huffed as he opened the door slowly. "Why did you have to be so incredible in bed?"

He burst out laughing. "Jenna. Jen!"

She stared up at his smiling face.

He leaned close. "I thought was you, I … wanted it to be you. I was asleep; she snuck in just to cause trouble. I didn't realize until you turned and ran out what was happening."

"What would have happened if I hadn't turned on the light?" she, wiping her nose on her sleeve.

"Nothing," He said tucking her hair behind her ear. "I rejected her a few days ago when her assistant propositioned me. Her assistant! Like I am not important enough to talk to in person, that's why she's trying to cause trouble."

Jenna winced and cleared her throat. "Sorry I called you a man-whore".

He pulled her up out of the car and into his arms. "Come on, I'll take you back to LA; team stunts are off for the next two days."

"I'll have to tell Scotty I'm leaving."

Rock closed her car door. "Call him on the way."

After grabbing her bag and crutches, he bent down and carried her piggy-back to his truck. She bit his ear playfully and whispered, "Will you be my man-whore tonight?"

He laughed. "Absolutely."

Jenna left Scotty a message on his cell as they exited the freeway on Gower Street and headed west to her teeny-tiny apartment. She gave Rock her keys and he opened the door to the studio, which offered only one room, one walk in closet and the world's smallest bathroom.

"I know it's small but it was all I could afford since I moved out here for stunt school."

"It's really, nice—nice and small," he teased.

With no room for any real furniture, she had a double bed that was also a sofa, one chair and a TV tray for a kitchen table. a small TV sat on a separate folding table. For as small as it was, the apartment was still pretty and feminine, decorated in shades of lilac and mint green, which Rock decided that he liked. Sitting on the bed, he looked into the one closet at about a hundred shoeboxes that lined the back wall. She handed him bottled water from the mini fridge, but he wanted a drink of another kind.

"Come here, you," he said, pulling her towards him.

Jenna sat down gently on his lap, put her arms around his neck, and let him kiss her with a fiery passion.

"The walls are so thin here," she whispered.

"So what!" He threw her down. She smiled up at him as he pulled her shirt and shorts off. Pulling his perfect penis out, she massaged it to life as he kicked off his sneakers and dropped his pants.

"Oh Rock, make me squeal like last time," she purred.

He growled. "I may do more than that."

They made love for the next hour, pounding the bed against the wall and being as loud as they possibly could until they exhausted each other.

"Let's go," he said, kissing her shoulder.

"I can't go another round yet."

"No, pack your things. We're going to my house."

"Really?" she said and jumped out of the bed.

He napped as she packed enough for two weeks, adding at least twenty pairs of shoes to her bag. Crawling over him, she woke him with a tickle from her long blonde hair on his nose. "I'm ready, sexy."

He loaded all her things without a comment into the SUV and they zoomed up to the top of hills. His ultra-modern house backed up to Runyon Canyon, a popular climbing park.

"Oh my gosh, I totally saw Bob Barker when I first moved here. He was walking up this very hill," she gushed as he pulled up. Spanish stucco lined the walls of the very masculine house.

"This place is great and big. You live here by your self?"

"Yes, I have a maid that comes in, but I'm on location most of the time, so it sits empty nearly all of the year." He smiled as he opened the door and let her in. Leather furniture graced the large living room. Defiantly a bachelor pad, she thought as she looked at the erotic black and white photos of naked female bodies that lined the mantle. Taking all her bags into the bedroom, he set them down and called her in into the room,

"Is this where all the magic happens?"

"There's a hot tub out there." He point to the French doors leading off the side of the bedroom.

"Are suits required?"

"Prohibited."

"Good." Sitting on the end of his bed, she rested her sore legs.

"Get naked and in the tub." He opened the French doors, took the cover off the hot tub, and started the jets. "I have to check my messages and mail."

"Take your time," she said as he placed his hand on her shoulder and squeezed. Slipping out of her clothes and into the tub, she sighed as the soothing heated water loosened the aching hamstrings. For twenty minutes, she let the water soak her shoulders. She thought how lucky she was to be here, in this lovely house with this wonderful, sexy man. A man she knew nothing about, pondered as the loneliness crept back in like a fog across an Irish sea. Watching him in the movies he was so different from the characters he portrayed, and even more different in person than she imagined. Where is he anyway, she wondered. He's been gone a long time and I am starting to prune. Just as she rose from the tub he appeared, bearing treats—chilled expensive champagne and luscious red strawberries. He placed them next to the tub and looked over her body.

"Thank you," she said as he handed her the Irish crystal flute. The bubbles tickled her nose making her laugh.

"Try this." He put a huge berry in her mouth and she bit down.

"Now sip."

"Oh that's awesome," she said, cheeks full of fruit.

He leaned over and kissed her strawberry-flavored tongue.

"Coming in?" she asked, splashing water at him.

"No, but you've been in there too long. Time to get out." Taking her hand, he helped her out and wrapped her in a large white, fluffy robe. She remembered the glass of champagne, brought it with her and followed him into the bedroom. Candles lit up the room, casting a warm, glowing light. She wondered what he had in mind when he went to closet. He brought to the bed what looked like three bandanas.

He placed the first over her eyes.

Jenna giggled nervously. "What are you doing?"

"Trust me." He slipped off the robe and placed her on the bed backside up. The second scarf he used to tie her hands together above her head to the wrought iron headboard.

"I don't know about this." Jenna swallowed and waited. Spreading her legs, Jenna winced both with vulnerability and a slight hint of proceeding pleasure. She shuttered as his long fingers smoothed over her tights and butt.

"Rock, wait, I don't do anal."

"I won't," he promised, his voice confident.

Running his digits down her inner thigh, he fingered her folds as she writhed into a pleasured frenzy. He continued until she was on the verge of a powerful orgasm. Struggling to hold off as long as she could, she felt the third bandana slide over her throat. Rock pulled the scarf back as he plunged his staff into her, cutting her air supply temporarily, and heightening the intensity by a thousand degrees. Jenna came as she had never experienced. Combining the blindfold, tied hands, and being choked to the point of unconsciousness gave her the orgasm of her life. Jenna allowed him unconditional control, completely letting go of her inhibitions and she finally came intensely. Thoughts of him trying to kill her and please her simultaneously flashed through her mind as came so hard she nearly passed out. Releasing the chokehold, he continued to take her from behind. Waves of pulsations flooded her physically. He was aflame inside her, and continued his pumping as she was still in an elation of the moment. Hammering her hard and fast, he tried to bring Jenna another round of pleasure.

"No more I can't," she pleaded with him. She came hard again as he pounded away.

"Rock, are you going to come?" she panted, struggling to free her hands, "I want to feel you." He pressed down on her rump and with two final thrusts into her he pulled out and shot his hot load onto her sweaty back yelling her name as he released his seed.

She lay waiting for him untie her hands and eyes for what seemed an eternity. Did he fall asleep?

"Rock? Untie me."

An ice-cold washcloth chilled her skin as he washed her, and then crawled up next to her, releasing her wrists so she could pull off the blind. He looked amazing with his sweaty skin glistening in the night light and his long hair wild like an animal. Jenna felt for her neck, amazed and confused by what just happened.

"I can't even look you in the eye that was so dirty."

"Then close your eyes and kiss me."

Jenna kissed his full lips and placed her head onto his chest, as he held her tenderly until they both fell asleep.

The next day they played all day at the beach, Rock hit the surf as Jenna relaxed working on her tan and catching up her sleep. Rock yelled to her to come down to the water's edge. Wading in slowly she shouted as cold waves crashed against their bodies. Dodging each one, they laughed together splashing and throwing seaweed at each other. Rock could not remember when he had laughed so hard. Jenna limped out of the water with Rock in tow.

"Your legs hurt?"

"Yes. I am going to sit down."

"Wait," Rock said and held her tightly. They shared a beautiful soft kiss. Stroking back her wet hair, Jenna tilted back her head, staring up into his deep brown eyes.

"I—you—I am so happy," he said showing her a rare moment of vulnerability.

"Me too, let's go back to the house."

After another round of amazing sex again they slept until around eleven p.m., Jenna got out of the bed and stumbled into the bathroom that was just off the bedroom. This bathroom is bigger than my whole apartment, she thought as she showered away sweat, sand, and sex. Leaning her head back to rinse her hair, she let water soothe her. She felt so contented, the warm water cascading down her sun kissed shoulders. Jolting head upright as the glass door opened to the shower, Rock joined her. Running his strong hands over her slippery body, he lathered her up as they kissed as they washed each other's body.

"Get pretty, we'll go eat." He turned off the water and helped her step out. She dressed, put on her face and fixed her hair all in a half-hour. Putting on a black velvet mini skirt and low cut matching top she sat on the bed and watched him pull on motorcycle boots, sexy black jeans, a tight black t-shirt, and leather blazer. Acting as if she did not notice the holster under his jacket, Jenna sat motionless on the bed. Why is he carrying a gun? Where is he taking her that he would need one? Jenna said nothing, simply she stood stepped into the wedge sandals and went out to the kitchen to wait for him. He liked the way the plat formed shoes made her legs look longer. Like a perfect gentleman, Rock opened her door and helped her into the large Escalade.

"Thank you, tiger."

He laughed slightly at her term of endearment. Jenna's laugh came out as a nervous blurb as she caught glimpse of the weapon under his coat. Pulling the truck out of the garage he watched her putting on her seatbelt. He rather liked the way she was so cute and kind, and not a mindless bimbo or gold digger like the rest of the L.A. women he dated. He like that she did not question him in bed and trusted him to push her limits sexually, but most of all he like that she was his whether she knew it or not.

Jumping in the driver seat, he cranked up the song In the Clouds by The Cult, as he zoomed down the hill to Hollywood Boulevard's Musso and Frank's. Late night always brought out actors, wanna-be starlets, Mafioso men and what appeared to be high-class hookers to the speakeasy-style restaurant and bar. It was as if the king had returned to the kingdom when Rock strode in the doors. Elderly Italian men greeted him warmly with kisses on both cheeks, actors shook his hands and women looked Jenna up and down as he escorted her through the place. He kept his hand firmly on the small of her back. She like the way he made her feel, as if she belonged to him, and that he paraded her through the restaurant like a man showing off his woman. An older waiter pulled out a chair to let them sit. Crisp white linens covered the table that was set with a small flickering candle.

"The usual table, Mr. Constantine."

"Good."

"And your drink, sir? As always?"

"Maybe my female friend her could decide?" Rock nodded to Jenna.

She grinned. "Red wine?"

"Bring the 1980 Timarosa." Rock leaned close to Jenna and began kissing her ear.

"Right away." The waiter scurried away as an elderly man came over to the table. Rock reluctantly pulled his lips from her ear.

"Ah, good to see you again sonny, and who might this Bella be?"

"Jenna, this is Uncle Nunzio."

The old, wrinkled, sun-ripened man took her hand, kissed it, and patted the top, in a way she found old-fashioned and sweet.

Winking, the old man said, "I'm not really his uncle."

Jenna squeezed his hand. "Pleasure to meet you, can I call you Nunzie?"

The old man roared with laughter. "I had a girlfriend once who called me that, you may remember an actress named Norma Jean?"

"Don't try to steal this one," Rock teased Nunzio.

The old man smiled. "She'd give me a heart attack with a body like that."

They all laughed as the old man strolled away and the waiter approached with the bottle, offering Rock a taste. Sampling it, he motioned for the waiter to pour for the both of them. The bitter dry wine made her face wrinkle.

"How do you drink this?" she said, coughing and choking at the same time.

Rock only grinned. "Drink it; it'll put hair on your chest."

"The only hair I want on my chest is yours rubbing against me as we do it all night long."

"I like how you think." He bit at her lip.

Four courses of seafood and steak; Jenna had not eaten this good since she moved to California.

"This is so wonderful," she cooed, allowing him to admire her hearty appetite.

"We'll burn off the calories later," Rock promised, looking at her with a devilish grin. She laughed with a cheek full of food.

Whispering into his ear, she told him, "That thing you did with the scarves, that was my first, you know, real time coming like that in my life". Her cheeks flushed with embarrassment.

"I could tell."

"Can I try it on you?"

He shook his head. "No, it's very dangerous, you have to know exactly how to do it."

"You really know how to do it," she purred in his ear. Pouring the last of the bottle between them, he slid his hand up her skirt nonchalantly. The other patrons had no clue what he was doing to her under the tablecloth. He talked coolly about the next scene as his fingers gorged into her. Jenna tried desperately to remain composed as blood rushed, swelling her womanhood. Rock nearly brought her to the brink of an unbridled explosion.

"Can I bring you another bottle?" the waiter appeared at the table.

"Yes!" she shouted as he gave her have a small orgasm. Jenna blushed deeply and chastised Rock, "You made me do that, right as the waiter came over here!" He looked at her and gave a wink.

"Let's go up to the bar."

As she slid onto the bar stool he stood next to her leaning one long arm on the brass railing. A young hunk in an Armani suit stopped by and they chatted for a while. Jenna sipped her tart wine silently as a sultry, red-haired barmaid came over to chat with her.

"Are you Rock's girlfriend?" the woman asked.

"No, we are just, um, working together on a location about two hours north of here." *Stupid, why did I say that? I sound like a dumb blonde.*

"He wouldn't have brought you here if you weren't his girl." The barmaid smiled and strolled away.

Jenna realized that Rock was feeling around his pockets for something. "What's wrong?"

"I left my phone in the truck. I'll be right back."

She stood. "I can get it, I need to stretch my legs, they're starting to cramp again."

He allowed her. "Thanks kiddo, I think it's in the console."

Rock gave her the keys she left her purse on the bar before heading outside to the alley where he parked his ltruck. She was pleased to be walking a little faster than the day before despite crutches. She opened the truck, leaned over the seat to reach in the middle to retrieve the black-cased phone, closed the door, and with one push on the remote set the alarm. She smelled, rather than felt a dirty palm cover her mouth, and someone pulled her deeper into the alley. Her scream of shock was muffled and fear raced through her mind. The attacker's jerking motions sent the phone and keys to the ground as the unseen person slammed her chest against the brick wall. Pinning her tightly to the wall with his forearm the man breathed heavily as he spoke in her ear.

"I got something for you, bitch."

Jenna struggled to turn her head enough to see the low-life thug His brown teeth were rancid and ugly.

"Don't look at me!" the attacker barked.

She knew he was undoing his pants. She tried to scream again but stopped when he wielded a knife in front of her face. She froze, her face a mask of terror.

"Did your girlfriend leave you?" the redheaded barmaid asked, running her fingers over Rock's shirt.

"She should have been back by now." He stepped from the bar stool, an impeding sense of danger washing over him. She's in trouble, I know it. In a moment, he was at the back door. There was no sign of her, not a person or thing in the alley. A faint, whimpering plea hit his ears, snapping his head around towards the rear. At first glance, Rock saw a figure facing the wall and the glint of the blade, and second glance he saw the bum trying to lift her skirt.

"Please stop, please", she squeaked out as the forearm on her shoulders crushed her arms and body tighter against the wall. With one solid blow, Rock pistol-whipped the attacker, sending him flying to ground. Before he could check on Jenna, the knife wielding man came at Rock with full force, his arm extended over his head. The knife blade directed downward at the other man. With easy effort, Rock blocked the attacking arm, grabbed hold of the man's wrist and twisted until a crunching sound proved he had snapped the man's arm like a twig. Finishing with a motorcycle boot kick to the ribs and head, Rock caught his breath as the attacker lay moaning on the bricks.

Approaching footsteps made Jenna's crouching body shake uncontrollably and she shield her head. The touch of a hand made her scream for help once again.

"Jen, kiddo it's me. Jenna!"

She shook like a scared Chihuahua pup as Rock scooped her into his massive arms. Still shaking and unsteady, Jenna clung to him as he placed her in front of the truck and went searching for the keys. He found the phone and keys next to the driver side tire. Hurrying back to her after picking up the items, he opened the door and settled her securely in the passenger seat. As he closed the door, the manager approached and questioned Rock about the incident. Jenna stared blankly at the men through the windshield as Rock attempted to pay for their drinks with a few hundred dollars, but the manager refused. The men shook hands and the barmaid appeared with Jenna's purse. By the time he was back into the truck, the shaking had stopped and Jenna became still as a statue. Her body was lost in shock. Silent tears streamed down her face as Rock climbed in and turned towards her.

"Did he?"

Hanging her head, she silently shook it from side to side.

"Oh, kiddo, I am so sorry, I should have never let you go out there alone." He wiped the tears from her cheeks as she kept her head down.

"Do you want to me to take you back to your apartment?"

Staring, lifeless as a doll, she could not answer.

Rock touched her cheek. "Do you want to stay with me?"

She nodded. His tires left tracks as they sped from the alley. They drove in sickening silence as Jenna stared out the window. The images blurred through liquid that filled her eyes and poured onto her lap.

She was the first to break the silence as they sat in the truck inside the garage.

"I should have been able to defend myself. I failed, everything you and Scotty taught me, I did not remember."

"Don't be hard on yourself; what we do is in a controlled, choreographed environment. He could have killed you."

"You saved me," she said flatly.

"I guess were even now," he told her in an even tone. A slight smile came to her face as he put an arm around her and moved Jenna from the truck into the house. She felt safe and secure in his tight embrace, he protected her, unlike her father who left her in the homeless shelter filled with filthy old men and predators.

"Rock, thank you from the bottom of my heart, for everything you have do for me. I appreciate every little and big thing you have done."

He held her at arms length, looked directly in the eyes, and kissed her forehead. "I have to be on set ten tomorrow morning, I think you'd better call Scotty and see what your schedule is." He said handing her phone out of her purse.

"I can't talk to him right now, I ..." Her cell phone beeped with a voice mail. The message was from Scotty telling her that she needed to be there tomorrow so the doctor could give her a checkup and possible release to come back to work.

"He wants me on set tomorrow at ten also."

Rock sighed. "It's late, let's go to bed."

Fright washed over her as images filled her head. No, not that!

"We need sleep. Only sleep. Come on," he assured her.

After separate hot showers, they climbed into bed together and Rock held her close with her head on his heart. The beating sounded like a drum in her ears as they lay silent, clinging to each other tightly, Rock wanting to protect her and Jenna wanting to feel safe, which she did.

"Thanks for coming to my rescue tonight." Jenna touched his chest.

"You're safe with me."

"I wished you would have shot that bastard." She said.

Rock let out his breath and agreed. "Me too."

He kissed her forehead and held her tight in his arms until she fell into a deep sleep. Rock stayed awake long after Jenna, thinking of the day's events. He remembered how she looked at him in her little apartment, the way her sexy eyes gazed at him over the glass as Jenna sipped the wine; how she trembled when he found her in the alley. He admired her hard work on the set and appreciated how unlike all the other L.A. women she seemed to be. Hollywood women in Rock's life only cared about money, power, and how thin they were. But Jenna did not ask for anything of him and gave all her trust to both on set and in bed, risking her own life to him, and yet she expected nothing in return. Her stirring in the bed next to him interrupted his random thoughts. She furrowed her brows worriedly and cried for help in her slumber.

"No, stop, someone help me … Rock, help me …" She tossed around in her nightmare and sobbed. "No, no, no …"

He could listen no more and reached for her.

Gasping, she sat straight and screamed. "He's after me!"

"Shhh. I'm here, Rock's here, you're okay." Rock pulled her to his chest.

She babbled wildly. "I was in the alley and he was going to shoot you and I tried to stop him and he pulled the trigger …"

"It was just a nightmare, I'm okay. You're fine now."

"I'm fine now." She repeated his words and drifted back to sleep. Rock closed his eyes and allowed his tired body to sleep as well.

Jenna awoke to the sound of the alarm buzzing loudly. Reaching over to turn it off, she looked at her lover who was asleep on his stomach, head buried under a pillow. Crawling out of bed, and into a hot shower, she washed and then dressed quickly, put on some light make up, and went to the kitchen to start coffee for him. When the pot was full, she carefully and slowly carried the streaming cup to Rock. It burned her hands as she set in on the nightstand. Watching the lines of his strong back muscles expand and contract with his breathing, she reached for and rubbed his smooth skin before leaning over and kissing his shoulder. So handsome and sexy, just like when she first saw him, playing a modern-day werewolf on screen. She was already in love with him from that first moment she saw him on film.

She knelt next to him. "It's black; is that how you take it?"

He pulled the pillow off his head, turned over, and sat up to sip the piping hot cup of joe.

"How are you feeling?" he asked her.

She shrugged her shoulder. "Still a little shook up, but I'll be okay. We need to hustle to get to the set on time. So get your butt out of bed, Constantine."

As he stood, she saw that he was sporting major morning wood, which made Jenna freeze in her tracks. He hugged her tightly from behind and she felt the hard on. Instead of exciting her, she completely freaked and started to shake.

"Please no, I'm sorry I can't."

He realized what his mistake. "No kiddo, no, I just wanted to hold you. I'm sorry."

"I thought you wanted to ..." she said half apologetically, half angry.

"Well, I always want to, but we can wait till you're ready."

She smiled at his sweetness, but reliving the events of the night before, kept her cold to his touch as he squeezed her shoulders. Rock hit the shower, leaving her standing alone in the bedroom feeling very afraid.

Arriving late to the set, they hurried to unload the truck as Scotty charged straight to them. Grasping her arm, and with fury in his eyes, Scotty pulled her aside. She started to shake as he berated her.

"What the hell were you thinking?" Scotty demanded.

"Sorry we're late, the traffic." She flinched.

"Are you trying to get us all fired?" he shouted.

Jenna shook her head. "We left on time."

Scotty's face flushed red. "I don't give a rat's ass about traffic!"

"I don't know what you're talking about," Jenna said. He was never this angry before and it confused her. Scotty threw a tabloid paper at her, open to an article whose headline read, *Private inside details from the set of Missy Manga's new movie. Stunt Girl reveals all.*

"I had nothing to do with this." She handed the paper back to him.

He looked at her with accusing eyes, nostrils flaring from his rage. After her injury, the horrifying attack, and her restless night, Jenna was at her breaking point. She pointed her finger to his chest and let loose.

"I can't believe you would even think I would have anything to with jeopardizing our careers. How long have we been friends? Two years, could you not give even a little credit? You have been my teacher and mentor and best friend since I started at stunt school and this the respect I get?" Tears welled up and she stormed away as Scotty stood battered as if he had just been hit by a tornado.

Rock put his arm on his friend's shoulder. "She couldn't have done this; she's been with your or me for the past few days. Did you really think she would?"

"No," Scotty sighed. "I guess I was I really harsh on her."

"After last night I'm not sure she can handle much more." Rock confided.

The other man frowned. "What are you talking about? Did something else happen?"

"She was attacked last night in the alley behind Musso's. Bastard nearly raped her." Rock balled his fists, remembering the attack.

Scotty was aghast. "What! Are you fucking kidding? What the hell was she doing in the damn alley?"

"She went out to my truck to get my cell phone."

"You sent her out to the alley alone?" Scotty seized his shirt with both fists.

Rock pushed him away. "I took care of the bastard, so take your hands off me ..." He felt the flush of anger. "Back off, Scotty!"

The two men began a stare off that was escalating quickly to violence.

Just as they were about to say something they would both regret, Tracy ran between the two, "Come quickly, you guys have got to see this!" They hurried to the parking area where Jenna's Volkswagen Fox sat parked. All tires were slashed, her windows busted out, the seat's fabric shredded, and the final insult was the large red spray painted letters on the side of the car. "WHORE".

Rock and Scotty watched, mouths agape as Jenna stood at the front of her car, face in hand sobbing heavily, ready to collapse.

"Holy shit." Rock was astounded.

"Do something," Tracy ordered them. Scotty went to Jenna. Leading her away, holding her up, he let her cling to him as she nearly fell to the ground. Rock went after Jared to contact the authorities and take care of all the arrangements to have her car towed away. In Scotty's trailer, Jenna continued to sob on his shoulder.

"Why Scotty, I have never done anything to anyone!"

"I know. I can't understand it. Now listen to me, I'm sorry I yelled at you. This really pisses me off." He shook his fist in the air.

Jenna fell heavily on the sofa. "I should be the one who's pissed, slipping in the shower, the accident on set, walking in and seeing Missy in Rock's bed, and now this ..."

"It's too much of a coincidence, wait, what did you say about Missy and Rock?" Scotty shot her a look.

Jenna explained choking on her tears, "I walked into his trailer. He was sleeping, and she slipped in his bed right before. Rock said that he thought it was me and kissed her right as I walked in. I turned and ran right out."

When Rock returned to the trailer, he told Scotty, "I need to see you outside."

Alone for the moment, Jenna went to the bathroom to splash water her face as she tried to compose her emotions.

Outside, Scotty crossed his arms and leaned on the trailer. "What's this about you and Missy in bed?"

"The little bitch set me up, to piss off Jenna or some shit. But, listen I just got a call from the manager at Musso's; he says he saw Missy's assistant in the alley throwing cash at the bum who attacked Jenna."

"So what do we do now?" Scotty asked. Rock looked at his friend, then looked carefully around before he spoke. "Watch our backs."

Three days passed without any incidents or problems and the stunt crew worked long, hard hours. Jenna was still sore but pushed through the pain and emotional trauma to finish the job. *One more shot and we'll be done for the day.* A heavy firearm battle between Missy's character and the nemesis was being set up and actors took their positions to start the scene.

"Do NOT point this at anyone," Scotty instructed the pain-in-the-ass starlet.

"Yee-haw!" She twirled the gun around her finger carelessly and everyone, grips, camera, sound, scrambled out of the way.

"God, they're fake bullets, what is everyone so freaked out about?" she scoffed as Scotty snatched the weapon from her like an enemy combatant.

"Do you want to kill yourself?"

Missy snapped, "I'm the star! Who are you to talk to me like that?"

"Just be careful please, they're just as dangerous as a real gun," he said through grinding teeth and trying his best to hold his professional composure. Jenna stood apart as she waited patiently to take her mark, away from the pop tart and her assistant, not wanting even to look in her direction. An hour and half into the shoot, Jenna was rigged into the wires and sent flying into the air with guns blazing. Take after take she delivered a perfect performance and after one final cut, the filming wrapped for the day. Unhooking her rigger cables, she went to the cases, checked the weapons, carefully placed them in a sealed silver metal box. One of Scotty's stunt men waited to take them from her. Then she was off to wardrobe for dinner, and hopefully, back to her tent. Not in the mood for company, she took her meal back to the temporary quarters, ate, and spread out on the cot, pulling out an old fashion magazine. Soon she was lost in photos of shoes and purses. After a few hours of isolation and reading the same articles she had a hundred times, Jenna decided to venture to Rock's trailer for a little late night nookie. She approached his door, dreaming of how she would straddle him, but Jenna was snapped out of the fantasy by moaning voices that could only come from one situation. Stomach pitching, she turned away. Thought teased and taunted her emotions she listened to the sexual situation noises. Maybe cause I did have sex with him this morning? Maybe he thinks I am I used goods. Maybe he is full of shit and he's with that red headed bar maid. It's not like we're dating ... *I guess he can screw whoever he wants and so can I.* She headed directly for Scotty's trailer, knocking softly as not to wake him if he was asleep.

"Who there?" Scotty called out.

"Me." Jenna reply softly.

Opening the door, she stepped in closed and locked it behind her. Scotty noticed right away, and wondered what she was up to.

"What are you doing up so late?" he questioned her, but she did not say a word, just stared with a look that made him swallow a lump in his throat. Taking the remote from his hand, she threw it on the table and pushed him onto the couch. Not wasting a minute, she crawled over his lap, grinding on him, kissing his face with passionate intent.

"Whoa, Jenna, what are you doing?" He tried to lift her off, but she held the back of the couch and pushed down against him. His resistance was half-hearted as the silky blonde hair brushed against his naked chest. Being on set and not dating anyone made him lonely and horny. Turning her efforts onto his neck and ear, she licked and sucked on it. He tried to stop her, he needed to stop her, but his thoughts were rational for about two seconds, before the male instinct kicked in. She hit his spot and sent him into full turned-on mode. It had been forever since he had any action, now the heat of her made him mad with lust. As she kissed his jaw, he closed his eyes and his staff went stone hard. His rough hands lifted the shirt over her smooth skin and he rubbed them roughly over her back as she pressed herself, grinding on his staff. The buzzing in his head made him lose every ounce of rationality as he took her breast into his mouth and teased her with his tongue. Suddenly she pulled back and Jenna stood before him as he sat point straight up at her from under the cotton fabric his boxer shorts. Lowering her shorts, she stood completely naked. Her body begging to be made love to. He threw her down on the couch and slid her under him into the right position to enter her. As he tugged the boxers in a clumsy attempt to get them off, she reached up and stroked his growing manhood. Tanned muscles in his completely ripped body pressed over hers as he took the condom from her hand and tore it open.

"You sure?" he asked. Not answering, she simply pulled his body between her legs in invitation and he rammed into her pink with tremendous force. He grunted wildly as he filled her with rapid pumps. Gorging into her tightness, Scotty felt his emotions overload as his body burned, and he gave her everything he could sexually. She moaned and squeaked as he thrust upon her his pent up tension. Panting like a rabid dog, he scooped his hands under ass, lifting her pelvis slightly and sending him into a vortex of orgasmic ecstasy. Bodies grinding against each other, she drug her nails down the length of his back, sending him to the brink. Unable to control it, he threw his head back and the dam burst inside him and flooded out. He bellowed loudly as the liquid filled the condom. Collapsing onto her, they lay intertwined in a heap of tangled flesh and they both gasped for air in the after-throes of a hot, sweaty, sex session. Untangling himself from her rocking body, he ran his hands in his dark, sweat soaked hair and slicked it back in exasperation. This crossed the line from friendship into some weird, unfamiliar territory and they both knew it. He spoke not a word, but went into the bathroom while Jenna hurried to dress. She left the trailer before he returned.

He's my best friend. Why did I do this? Guilt and pleasure mixed in a strange brew of emotions that stuck in her throat.

"Hey, I've been looking all over for you." She felt Rock's firm grip over her shoulders. "I hoped you would come to my trailer. I got a new porno and I was watching it thinking of you."

The blood rushed to her head as the dizziness overwhelmed her senses.

"I need to be alone."

She ran away, leaving him confused. *Oh no. This is so bad.* She retched, her stomach contents spilling from her in a sickening rush. *I thought there was someone with him …* Jenna took a few deep breaths. *What did I do?* She just seduced her boss and best friend and regretted it instantly. Jenna headed to Jared's trailer to quit.

Tracy answered instead of the director. "What the hell happened?"

"I need a drink."

"Come in, Jared's gone, it's just me. Here." Handing her a tiny bottle of whiskey, Tracy waited while Jenna downed it with one gulp.

"I screwed up, literally. I went by Rock's and I heard him with some one else. I was furious! I went and I … Oh, Tracy. I had sex with Scotty."

Tracy's jaw fell open and Jenna helped herself to another bottle. Grabbing one for herself, Tracy downed hers just as quickly.

Jenna choked from the liquor and wiped her lips. "Rock wasn't with anyone else. He was watching porn."

"Hell, you thought you had problems before." Tracy dropped to a chair. "You know how tight they are. They act like brothers."

"I am so stupid, what should I do now? They both mean the world to me, I need to go tell Scotty it was a mistake and I'm sorry and come clean to Rock. Thanks for the drink," Jenna said miserably.

Tracy took the bottle from her. "Sure, come back and stay with me tonight when you're done."

"Okay, thanks."

They hugged like sisters before Jenna left. Walking around for a few minutes to gather her thoughts and apologies, Jenna thought out exactly what she was going to say to both men. At Scotty's trailer, Jenna did not bother to knock and walked right in to find the place quiet and dark.

"Scotty?" she whispered. With no response, she crept back to the bedroom to wake him.

She heard the whoosh of the object just before it made hard contact with her back. Jenna spun around. In the darkness, a figure rushed at her swinging again the unknown object and this time smacked her dead in the face. Ripping flesh burned as her lip spilt in two, sending salty hot liquid into her mouth. Remembering to defend herself this time, Jenna lifted her arms as the hard stick came down on her. With one good punch from her, the weapon went flying. They fought, crashing over everything in the darkness. She tumbled and ducked until the figure pinned her against the wall and the attacker choked her tightly. Jenna pounded her arms in a downward thrust, loosening forearms from her neck. She was loose, and turned to run from the trailer, but a hand gripped her hair, and sent her into the wall. Jenna faded into the black of unconsciousness as another blow hit her head.

As the two men walked back to Scotty's trailer, Rock and his friend talked civilly to each other. Their fight forgotten, the men were now discussing Jenna, and Scotty listened as Rock spoke.

"You know I really like her, and I know you two are good friends. I think I want to date her seriously."

Scotty debated telling Rock what happened between them. "Listen, she is my good friend, and I know she really likes you. Give her a chance, she's a real sweetheart. What happened between us meant nothing."

"What do you mean?" Rock stopped and frowned. As Scotty began to answer, Rock looked past him. A shimmer of dark liquid glistened in the moonlight on Scotty's white trailer door.

"Look!" Rock said.

They approached the door and Scotty reached in and flipped on the outside light.

"What the ..." Scotty cursed as he found the trailer in shambles. It looked like a good fight. Blood spattered in odd patterns across everything from the door back to the bedroom.

Standing in shock, they surveyed the mess.

"Jenna's shoe. She was here. Someone took her," Rock said as he clutched her purse.

"Who would, why would they ...?" Scotty tried to understand as a rumbling of people's feet and shouting turned their attention to the outside commotion. Rock jumped from the trailer into a wall of searing heat. The scorching air covered the two and they heard people screaming. More than a few ran toward the Chinatown set. Glowing orange illuminated the night sky as the fire burned bright enough to make it daytime.

Choking smoke filled her lungs and she awoke suddenly, gulping in a deep breath of black smog. Struggling for air, Jenna coughed and gasped as she tried to orientate to the surroundings. Jenna was not at all sure where she was; all she knew was that she was in a smoked filled room and time was running out. Along the floor, she moved forward, feeling blindly as the burning seared the lining of her throat and lungs. Not wasting any energy on a scream, she felt for the plywood of the floor and ran smack into a wall. The unavoidable heat singed her hand. Go opposite direction, her brain told her. Crawling fast, she scrambled around fifty feet until she came to another wall. Cooler to the touch, she followed along the wall until she felt something metal. Door hinge. *Yes*, she thought. Going across the wood, she cautiously touched for a handle. The metal knob was cool to the touch, but freedom escaped her, as the handle would not turn.

"No, no, no" she cried out. Smoke and heat overcame her, until she could do nothing else but lay her aching head against the hard wood floor. In a last ditch, effort she prayed Rock would rescue her. *Please if you can hear me, find me, there is not much more time.*

"Check all the sets! I just know she's in there," Rock over the sound of the raging fire. Knowing his intuition was usually spot-on, Rock turned to Scotty. Scotty nodded to his friend without question. Panic and fear washed over the two as they rushed towards the doors of the fake storefronts as the inferno engulfed most of the structures on the set. A faint siren wailed in the far distance as the volunteer fire department hurried toward the set as Rock kicked in doors, screaming Jenna's name.

She heard his voice in the distance. Trying her best to communicate to him, her voice would not make enough noise so she banged on the door with her foot. Soon the smoke and heat overcame her, weakening her body. Jenna's strength was fading rapidly.

"No luck?" Scotty said as he approached Rock. He shook his head no, and the fire raged around him.

"We gotta get out of here," Scotty pleaded with his friend.

"I know she's here, I don't know why, but Scotty we have to look one more time." Rock went back to check on one last door as Scotty followed behind, begging him to leave.

"Did you hear that?"

A faint repetitive banging came from a fake door. Both of the men hurried toward the sound.

Heat tortured her body as the flames licked a foot away from her back, dancing their dangerous game towards her.

"Kiddo!!" Rock yelled over the roar of the fire.

"Help, Rock, Scotty, please … can't open the door." She coughed.

Scotty pointed at the entrance. "She's in here, I can hear her."

"Get away from the door!" Rock said.

"Rock …" Her voice faded as the smoke and heat took a toll. With one determined kick, the door blew off the hinges, sending thick smoke billowing out of the doorway and temporarily blinding their view. Running in anyway, Rock felt around on the floor for her while yelling her name. The dense wall of smoke choked and strangled him. Panicked, he moved blindly around in the heat and smoke. Rock searched frantically. Suddenly, his hand felt a soft lump of flesh. *Got her!* he thought but was sickened when her body was limp in his arms.

"No, she can't be! Oh no, kiddo." With no more time to think, he dragged Jenna to the doorway while burning embers stung like mad bees on their skin.

"Get an ambulance!" Rock screamed to Scotty who grabbed Rock and pulled him out of the doorway. Unable to feel a pulse, he laid her on the ground and shouted at her to wake up.

Jenna felt as if she was floating away from her body. The voices faded as she drifted further toward the illuminated tunnel.

"Jenna, Jenna! Stay with me, honey. Oh god Rock, she's slipping!" Scotty's voice cracked, his eyes were red-rimmed and wet.

"I'm not ready to go yet; I want to go back, back to Rock and Scotty." She felt, rather than heard her voice.

"It's not your time," a most beautiful voice of her mother spoke softly to her.

Paramedics forced the men away took over.

"She's flat lined. No pulse. Start compressions." A female EMT started CPR on the fragile body of Rock's lover and Scotty's friend. Scotty held his head in his hands weeping while Rock pounded his first the side of the ambulance and put his head down against the metal van.

"I have a pulse, we got her back," the female paramedic shouted.

Both men's heads popped up from their bowed position. Rushing to her side, the men stared in amazement as she opened her eyes, coughed hard and spoke gruffly from soot-filled lungs.

"The light it was so beautiful. I had to come back … wasn't my time."

"Don't try to talk, save your strength," Scotty pleaded with her.

Delirious and near fainting, she gazed at Rock. "Why, why did they do this?"

"Who did this?" he asked, leaning next to her mouth.

Jenna's raspy voice spoke quietly in his ear. "Two females, I didn't see them." She closed her eyes in exhaustion.

Rock tried to make sense of her statement. Females?

"You guys saved me." she whispered, and she fell unconscious again.

"We're taking her to Riverside General. Her burns are minor but the smoke inhalation is serious. You should let me check you out," the kind EMT offered to Rock.

"I'm fine. Thanks for helping her."

The woman touched his forearm before jumping into the back of the rig. As countless people milled around dosing flames and fire, the ambulance took Jenna away from the two men she loved with all her heart.

Scotty spoke in a low tone, "No one saw anything. Emergency meeting at Jared's trailer. Let's go." Rock was glad for the distraction of worrying about Jenna.

As the two walked, Rock spoke to his friend. "She didn't see them." Scotty looked at him.

"There were two ... girls," Rock told Scotty.

Scotty flexed his fists. "Damn it!"

"Listen up people, the show must go on, we have budgets and a schedule and a studio who is spending millions to get this film made and it will be finished ... on time!" the director shouted furiously. Rock kept his arms crossed, as he himself was infuriated at the fact that Jenna's life did not matter as much as the bottom-line and that he was apart from her right now when she needed his protecting.

After the briefing, they made their way to the parking area and jumped into Scotty's large luxury BMW sedan. They rode in silence, Rock pressed fingers against the bridge of his nose trying to stop the growing headache as Scotty drove and checked his voicemail.

As Scotty drove into the emergency entrance parking lot Rock stared straight ahead. "Whoever is responsible will pay." Scotty said.

Rock's response was more severe. "They'll pay, with their last breath."

His cell phone rang and Scotty snatched it from the seat. "I have to take this I'll meet you inside."

Inside, a nurse directed Rock to the examination room where they took Jenna. Finding his girl lying in the bed, he stood looking at her sleeping like an angel with soot-covered cheeks. Tiny burns marks on her a hands and arms looked like someone took a red marker and dotted her. It broke his heart to see her like this. *There just something about her*, he thought, recalling the first time he saw her on set listening to Scotty's direction, smiling as she turned and looked in his direction, eyes sparkling like gem stones, blonde hair shining like gold in the morning light. He knew she idolized him, but did not want to be involved with anyone, nor let his guard down with another woman especially one this young, but something about her stirred his soul, awoke him from the heartless one-night stands and nameless women. Rock sat on the edge of the bed, watching her brow furrow as it did when she was having a nightmare. He brushed the dirty hair from her face and smoothed his knuckle down her cheek. Wanting her spunky personality to awake and make him laugh again, he ran a fingertip over her dry, spilt, lips.

A nurse coming into the room broke his deep concentration.

"Are you her husband?"

"No."

"Next of kin?"

"She's my girl." He lifted Jenna's hand.

"Visiting hours are over, we have to admit her now."

"When will she be released?" Rock asked.

The nurse only shrugged. Too soon to say, come back in the morning."

Just as Rock started to walk out, Scotty entered and hurried right to Jenna. He picked up her hand and stroked it.

"She's going to be fine," the nurse said, "we gave her a sedative. She'll be out till morning."

Rock crossed his arms. "We'll need security to stand guard. This was no accident."

"I can call them for you," the nurse offered.

"I am staying with her." Rock was not to be moved.

"Then I'll come get you in the morning. I have to get back to the set." Scotty patted Rock's shoulder and walked away, leaving Rock sitting with his stunt girl.

Morning came quickly as Rock slept in next to Jenna in an empty hospital bed. A sound, rustling, movement. Rock turned just as Jenna opened her eyes. She looked wildly around the room, confused. He got up quickly, went to her side, and sat on the bed. She opened her mouth to speak but nothing would come out of her throat. Jenna closed her eyes in frustration. He poured her a glass of water from the Styrofoam pitcher next to her bed. Holding up the cup to her lips, he steadied her with one hand as she drank.

"Thank you," she managed as her dry throat was quenched. "Was anyone else hurt?"

"No."

Relief came over her worried brow as she took more water from him. "How did you find me?"

"I just did." He smiled at her.

"I remember floating over my body, and I heard you calling my name. I wanted to come back."

"I am glad you did," he said hugging her tightly.

The doctor interrupted the lover's moment. "Can you give me a minute?"

"I'll be outside," Rock told her and she nodded at him.

He walked to the waiting room and helped himself to a fresh pot of coffee. Rock sipped the streaming liquid as he rubbed the back of his neck. What a week. This was by far one of the most challenging one he had ever had. He smiled at the best part, waking up to find her in his bed. The smile faded quickly as he thought of the worst, thinking she was dead, that he was too late to save her, just like he was too late to save the only other woman he ever loved his mother. Once again he pushed that thought out of his mind and tried to make sense of it all and what was next? But there it was he loved her. Damn, he thought, I'm in love. Stepping back into the hall, he noticed Scotty hurrying toward him.

"Hey. What's the word on the set?" Rock asked.

"Listen, no one knows how it started, and no one seems to know where Missy or her assistant were at time it started."

"We can't let on that we suspect anything. If we are wrong, we could be facing serious charges. And we would never work in this town again."

"They want to sweep this all under the rug. They are calling it and accident and have not said anything about Jenna or her injuries. By the way how bad is she?"

"She'll be fine, smoke inhalation, a few small burns. She's one tough cookie."

"I know I made her that way," Scotty joked to try to relive some of Rock's stress.

"I am going to find out who did this and take care of it. You want to know about it?"

"It's best I don't," Scotty said and walked away from Rock and into Jenna's room. Rock made a quick call and joined his friend who was conversing with the doctor outside Jenna's room.

"She's taken in quite a bit of smoke, and there's some injury to the lining of her lungs, but I think that with plenty of liquids and rest, she will be okay. I'll be releasing her today, if everything looks okay." The doctor gave Rock a prescription and told him to have it filled either at the hospital or on the way home. Just as the doctor walked away, a little man in a cheap brown suit weaseled passed them, peeked into Jenna's room and looked around. Scotty and Rock shared a look of where the hell is he going and where the hell is security. Moments later, the man slipped into her room and they were right behind him.

The man stood in front of Jenna as she held the folded blue sheet up to her chin.

"You Jenna O'Fallon?" the little chubby man demanded.

"I am. Why?" Jenna looked beyond the man to her two heroes.

"Who wants to know?" Rock asked.

"Consider yourself served," the man said, scrambling past the friends and out the door. Jenna opened the blue-lined legal document and her shoulders shook with silent tears. Scotty snatched the paper from the bed after she put her hands over her face.

"Missy Manga is suing her for defamation of character in regards to the tabloid article. $1.25 million in damages are being sought." Scotty slapped the paper on the tray table.

Jenna turned away from them and sobbed.

"Don't cry kiddo; you're breaking my heart," Rock told her.

"I had nothing to do with that article, and I don't even have a hundred twenty-five *dollars* in the bank. It's not fair." Her words were broken by sobs. Rock rubbed her back as the doctor came in and handed her a release form to sign. Rock followed the doctor out of the room to where he told him what she would need for the next few days.

Scotty pulled an armchair to her bedside and sat, taking Jenna's hand. "Sorry, honey, I have more bad news. You were fired. Missy wouldn't agree to come back on set unless you were terminated, and the studio put too much pressure on Jared to keep production going. The fire caused a big setback, which made them go over budget and they've already invested a bundle in this project."

"But ..." She didn't understand.

"That's just the way Hollywood works."

Jenna twisted the bed sheet in her hands. "Did they fire you and Rock also?"

"No," Scotty told her.

She sighed and dropped her hands. "Oh, I couldn't live with myself if you guys lost your jobs because of me. I swear I never wanted any of this to happen."

Scotty leaned close so only she could hear. "I know and Rock knows, but he doesn't know what happened between us and I think it should stay that way."

Jenna nodded in agreement. He smiled at her and they both broke out in an embarrassing laughter. Rock entered the room and asked, "What's so funny?"

"I'd rather laugh than cry right now." Jenna said, smiling tersely. "Surprise, I was fired."

Rock's heart filled with tenderness. It was only a hint of a smile, but it was good to see it on her face.

"The doctor has released you. Soon as you get dressed we can go."

Jenna's smiled faded to a frown, "I don't have any clothes. They cut them off me in the emergency room. I loved that outfit. And my shoes … I don't know what happened to my shoes."

The nurse came in and helped her to the shower as her men moved to a waiting room. Like salt into an open wound, Jenna felt the humiliation of having to hold the hospital gown closed and her paper booties rustling along the marble floor of the lobby. She was mortified that it was all she had to wear; there was no dignity in hospital attire.

"A hundred pairs of shoes in my closet and I'm wearing paper booties!"

The three walked in silence, except the noise of paper shoes shuffling. By the time they made it to the car, the booties had disintegrated, Jenna was sure she'd die of shame.

"Want me to take you back to your car? Oh, sorry." Scotty blushed a little at his faux pas as he remembered that her car was destroyed. The floodgates of tears opened again and the two men looked at each other in dismay. "No car, no shoes, no job, no dignity," she sobbed as she climbed into the back seat and laid her head on the seat. Only her sniffles let them know she was in the vehicle.

"Here kiddo." Rock handed her some McDonald's napkins that he pulled out of Scotty's glove box. I'm blowing my nose in French fry grease, she thought dismally. It wasn't but a few miles till she became groggy.

"I think she's out again. I don't know what they gave her, but it's working." Scotty checked his rear view mirror to see her fast asleep across the back seat. "You and I both need to be back on set at eleven in the morning for the police report and a production meeting. Let's all crash at my place tonight, it's closer to the set, and we can get a decent night's sleep. Beside, I don't think she wants to go back to Hollywood and be alone. She can stay at my place tomorrow. She'll be safe down there, no one on set knows where I live."

"Good idea. I can get some surf time in, clear my head," Rock agreed.

Pulling up to Scotty's beachfront estate on the Pacific Coast Highway in Surf City, Huntington Beach, they were lost in though. The garage doors opened to the lower level of a three-story house that boasted an unblocked view of the roaring brown ocean. Scotty carried her things while Rock woke Jenna and helped her out of the car into the classically decorated beachfront estate. Jenna curled up on the couch, yawned, and fell back asleep. After throwing a blanket over her, Scotty set the alarm on the highly fortified house. Rock and Scotty changed into wet suits in the garage and with boards under arms walked the across the street to the beach. As they had done hundred of times before, the two friends spent the rest of the morning and afternoon in the ocean trying to catch the ideal wave.

In the late afternoon, they found Jenna still sleeping and prodded her to wake for dinner from the local pizza parlor.

"I'm not hungry," she protested, laying her head back on the couch cushion.

Rock was adamant. "You need to eat. When was the last time you had ate?"

Jenna shrugged sleepily. Rock brought her a plate and sat next to her, set it in her hands, and switched on the Lakers game. The cheesy pizza smell filled her nose and she quickly regained her appetite. After eating three slices and half of Rock's lasagna, Jenna felt too stuffed to move and placed her head on his lap until half time. It was early yet, but they were all exhausted from the events of the last evening. Jenna took her meds and zonked out on the couch. Rock went to the guest room where he always crashed when with his friend. Scotty retired to his third floor bedroom that opened out to the patio and dropped his tired body on his king size bed. The sound of the ocean lulled each of them to sleep and they slumbered like hibernating bears for more than ten hours.

Up by seven, the guys both hit the ocean for an early morning surf session. Around nine, they felt much less stressed and enjoyed the smell of fresh coffee brewing, thanks to the automatic timer Scotty had set. Jenna lay snoring loudly on the couch. Looking at Rock, Scotty laughed that she sounded like she was sawing logs in her sleep.

"She's a keeper," Rock agreed.

"She snores loud as you," Scotty joked with his friend.

Rock threw a towel at him. "Let's roll, traffic will be heavy today."

"Think she'll be okay?" Scotty said. "Rock did not want to leave her but they had no choice they both had to be on set for some critical re-shoots.

"She'll be fine, I arranged for someone to stand guard outside, keep his eye on her," Rock assured him. "She can't go too far with out a car. My brother is discrete; she will not know she is being guarded "Good deal, let's roll."

Waking up around eleven a.m., Jenna found herself tangled in the hospital gown. She stood up, tore it off, and threw it onto the floor. A note on the coffee table in caught her eye.

Hey kiddo, my sister left some clothes in the spare bedroom. There are all kinds of shops two blocks down—go buy some thing to wear and by the way, you snore like a lumberjack.—Scotty.

Next to the note were seven one hundred dollar bills. Normally she would have been ecstatic to have this much money to go shopping, but she felt like such a charity case. Besides, she did not snore or so she liked to think. Jenna felt refreshed after the hours of peaceful dreamless sleep. Deciding a shower would be in order, Jenna stepped in to the bathroom of the guest bedroom dragging her pink and black duffle bag behind her. She was not sure how one of the two men managed to find it, but she was grateful that she had her own shampoo, razor, makeup, and her can't-live-without favorite curling iron. Damn no clothes, what the hell happened? Oh yeah they were in the car. Damn. My Volkswagen, I worked so hard to pay that car off. I loved that car. Jenna allowed herself a small pity party, while she showered, shaved, and put on her face. Good therapy she thought. Nothing like fresh makeup to make me feel better. She tried to cover some of small burn marks with concealer but it was useless. There were simply too many. Well, she sighed, at least my hair was not burned off. I have to think positive.

Rummaging through the closet, Jenna found a 'Someone in California loves me' tee shirt, a mini skirt in hot pink, and a pair of flip-flops that were a size too big.

They will just have to do, she thought, She had no other alternative.

Walking down the Pacific Coast Highway the down town was only two blocks. Not sure why but she felt safe here. The sun shone down warming her as she walked along the sidewalk towards the shops. She filled her head with images of Rock and the best times of the past week and pushed out the bad images as she had trained her mind to do over the years. Oddly she didn't feel alone, but was not scared. The sidewalks filled with tourists and surfers heading towards the beach and boardwalk. Oh, these shops are so cool, she thought, her mind instantly off death attempts and concentrated on trendy shorts, bikinis, and souvenirs. Jenna browsed in several places before buying herself bras and panties, three tank tops, shorts, more flip flops in her size, a super cute purse with wedges to match, and a sundress in lemon yellow with tiny red roses printed on it. It was a great day, full of bargains in every store. After she had exhausted herself shopping for two hours, Jenna walked slowly, wincing as the bags handles cut in to her hands. The two blocks to the beach house seemed much longer than when she had first walked it this morning.

I still have three hundred bucks left, she thought as she counted her change, after dropping the packages in the guest room where Rock has slept the night before. After putting on a new bikini and keeping on the cute pink skirt, she slipped into new-jeweled crusted flip-flops and went back to the pier to watch the ocean. Standing by the railing of the pier, she watched the old and young interact as they all enjoyed the sounds of a Caribbean band that played in the afternoon air. Most of her worries and stress ebbed away with the tide and she decided to go frolic in the waves for a while. The water was cold and cleaning to the soul. *Amazing how the ocean can wash away the hurt and bad emotions.* Till the salt stung her wounds, of course and she went back to the beach and toweled her skin dry. Here, on the beach she felt safe and watched idly the waves, which reminder of the day her and Rock spent at the beach. Maybe I can find some shells she thought and got up brushing the sand from her bottom. Walking along the cold wet sand at the waters edge, Jenna nearly jumped out of her skin as a beached sea lion barked at her when she nearly stepped on it, shaking her back to reality. She laughed and kept moving. A volleyball rolled to her feet and she stopped, scooping it up and throwing it to a shirtless young player. He was tall as she was petite, and he eyed her curiously.

"What the hell happened to you?" he asked looking, at her scarred body.

"I'm a stunt girl. It comes with the territory," she told him, not wanting to explain about the fire and attempt on her life.

"Gnarly." The buff dude said to her, Jenna thought as she stood on the sidelines, watching the game. From the worst day to the best day, how could I be so lucky to be alive?

She sighed, and breathed deeply the salty sea air. "God, I love this place." It was nothing like the fast pace of L.A. The beach gave her a laid back no-worries attitude. "I have to tell the guys about this tonight."

Heading up to the boardwalk to get some lunch at the outdoor café on the beach, Jenna noticed some street kids watching her order from the waiter. She signaled to them to come over to her table, which did not please the waiter.

"You guys hungry?" Jenna asked them. They looked sheepishly at her. Two girls and an adolescent boy hesitated, then nodded. "Order what ever you want, it's on me."

They ordered a teenage banquet, burgers and fries.

"Why you being so nice?" one girl said from behind her bangs as she wolfed down French fries and a coke.

"I know what's like to be hungry," Jenna told them. She thought of the nights sleeping in her car, her stomach rumbling from the emptiness, the pains cramping her insides. How she hoped Scotty would remember to bring in bagels to the school in the morning so she would have something to eat. She saw that hungry look in these kids eyes and it broke her heart.

"Thanks, lady." They had eaten like vultures on a carcass and finished before Jenna was able to eat half her oriental chicken salad. It lifted her spirits being able to help someone else less fortunate then her. In that moment, she decided that someday she would make a difference and help people. Jenna never wanted anyone to feel the way she had, alone, no where to go, no one to turn to. Her eyes welded up with tears. Brushing them away before the kids noticed she smiled, choking back the rest.

After eating and talking to the street kids for a while, Jenna traveled back to the ocean to wash more of the negativity of the days before off her skin. Like a baptism, she dipped in the frigid waters repeatedly as the surf washed against her body, cleaning her soul. No wonder Scotty lives here. This place is magical. If I could afford it, I would move down here from Los Angeles, some day, I will live here.

"Yikes!!' Something slimy brushed against her, sending her into a run to the shore. "Seaweed, gross!"

She trudged out of the wake and sat down on the wet sand, sun blinding her as it hung over the horizon. Genius that she was, Jenna never considered buying sunglasses. Well, I can go get them now. Taking the money from her skirt, she walked to the shops, bought a pair of cool oversized sunglasses, and headed before making her way to the house. On the street, she stopped at a small corner market. The sweetest little couple ever greeted Jenna as she walked in and it was another hour before they stopped talking to her. They told her they were from the Midwest also. The cute elderly Italian couple said they moved from Detroit over sixty years ago and both of them knew Scotty well. The woman, a cheerful, small charmer gave her all the necessary ingredients to cook the evening's dinner. The little bent-over woman gave her specific instructions to make the perfect Italian meatballs.

"To be honest, I've never made anything like this before." Jenna was embarrassed at her lack of cooking skills.

The woman reassured her. "Oh, little Bella, you follow my recipe and you will have the best meat sauce."

She gave them hugs as if they were her own grandparents, and promised to follow instructions faithfully. After carrying the brown paper bags into the house, she unloaded the contents on to the kitchen counters and proceeded to start preparing dinner. As the sauce simmered, Jenna showered the sand off and put on her new sundress, then cleaned up the house and set the table.

Scotty's home phone rang but Jenna did not answer it. It seemed too intrusive.

"I know you're listening to this so pick up," his voice said through the machine.

She put the phone to her ear. "Hi, how's your day going?" Jenna inquired.

He sounded tired. "Rough, it's not easy without you. But we'll be back around six-thirty."

"I went shopping and to the beach and now I'm making dinner." Jenna pulled open a box of spaghetti.

"Geez, calm down. Don't overdo it. Do you want to go back to the hospital?"

Jenna was actually very sore. "Okay, but I feel much better, and I wanted to thank you for everything you have done for me, I promise to pay you back all your care."

"Please! I'll take it out of your next paycheck," he teased her.

She laughed. "Don't be late, or you'll eat this fabulous dinner cold." As she hung up the phone, Jenna sat down on the couch. Now she was feeling a bit woozy. Moments later, she was fast asleep.

"Oh no!" Jenna flew from the sofa to the kitchen and looked at the clock on the stove. After six! Rushing around, she prepared the salad, started the water for the pasta, and checked the simmering sauce and meatballs. To her great relief she had slept only ten minutes and everything was cooking just fine.

"Everything looks perfecto!"

Scotty's pantry had a collection of place mats so; she lined the table and found some blue and white candles in the cabinets. Jenna placed a few seashells she found out on his patio in strategic places for the centerpiece. The strong scent of garlic bread filled the kitchen, as it baked in an oven that looked as if had never been used. *Bachelor!* She rolled her eyes and went to fix her face and hair. Jenna laughed as she put the finishing touch on her makeup. I feel like I have a date with two men, she thought.

Kinky, she laughed aloud and went to the living room to turn on the stereo, which had so many buttons she was almost afraid to try. Somehow, Jenna succeeded in making the CD player play U2's latest songs. Six-forty-five rolled around with no sign of the men, while Jenna paced with nervous excitement. Opening a bottle of Italian merlot, she placed it carefully on the table and straightened the silverware, jumping with joy when she finally heard the creaking of the garage door. The men looked a little weary as they staggered into the house breathing in the great smells.

"What's all this?" Rock asked her with a smile.

Jenna smiled proudly. "I cooked."

"Smells great, I'm starved," Rock told Jenna as he kissed her cheek. Scotty lifted the lid and dipped his finger in the sauce for a quick taste.

"You guys stink, go shower," she ordered, snapping a towel at Scotty's ass.

Jenna turned her head as the two men made a show of smelling themselves.

"You're right." Rock motioned to his friend, and the two men walked out of the kitchen, Scotty went to the master bathroom and Rock to the one off the guest rooms. Fifteen minutes later they emerged to take places at the table, clean shaven and smelling much better. Jenna served the hungry men. Placing the steaming dishes of food onto their plates she piled the pasta on and pouring the sauce over it, she felt mothering. Scotty made a toast in Italian and they drank, ate, and talked about the day.

"Get me more bread, woman," Rock joked with her.

"Yes master!" Jenna was very happy to do his bidding.

As she went into the kitchen, Rock spoke to Scotty. However, his friend was busy drinking out of the water pitcher and couldn't answer.

"It's a little salty," Rock said, wrinkling his nose.

"That's an understatement!" Scotty laughed and drank more water.

"What's so funny?" Jenna wondered as she appeared in the doorway.

"Nothing," Scotty snickered.

"Sa—lty," Rock fake-coughed under his breath.

Jenna crossed her arms. "Oh? Why didn't you just come out and say it's awful? It's terrible, isn't it?"

Rock tried to keep a straight face. "It's not that bad."

Scotty rolled his eyes. "Can I have some more water?"

Rock put his hand on hers and squeezed. "Good Try, kiddo." He and Scotty lost their battle and erupted in laughter.

Jenna was disappointed that she failed in her cooking adventure that her stomach closed and she pushed food around her plate, barely eating. After a while, she gave up on eating and shooed the men away while she cleaned and did the dishes. On the patio on the top floor, Scotty grabbed two beers from the mini fridge behind the bar. Rock took one and leaned over the railing to watch the ocean in its endless cycle, crashing to the shore non-stop. Joining them on the patio, Jenna grabbed another round of drinks for all of them. Rock, teasing, held the drink away until she gave him a kiss. Two beers and a pain pill later, Jenna was feeling no pain. Drunk, she went to sit on the lounge chair and missed.

"Someone can't handle her liquor," Scotty mentioned to Rock.

"I am fine, I'm fine, I can walk, I can do stunts, and I can shoot big guns." Jenna voice was a thick slur as she stumbled to the lounge chair. It took two attempts to sit and the men found it greatly amusing. In her drunken state, Jenna stared coldly at them.

"You think I'm a joke? I worked hard to be a stunt man—woman—person. And—I never gave up. I am good and nice and despite someone trying to rape me and kill me, I am still standing." She sat on the floor pointing her finger. "And let me tell you guys something ..."

With a shared look, they waited patiently as she continued.

"I love you guys, you're the best friends I every had, you're good and nice and generous. I'm going to prove to you that I am going to make something out of myself." She swigged from the bottle and continued.

"You are going to be proud of me someday. You'll see my name in lights, Jenna O'Fallon, super star!"

Rock got up as she spilled beer on her dress. "Okay, stunt girl, give daddy the bottle."

She frowned as he took it from her and pulled her up to her feet.

"I need one more ... like a lady," she said.

"Give her one more, I haven't laughed this hard all week." Scotty said as Rock went and got the last beer from the fridge.

"Last one. You got more down stairs?"

"Not sure, I'll go check." Scotty went off downstairs and Jenna yelled.

"Hurry back, Scooter!"

After the Italian stallion left, Jenna crawled up on her lovers lap and tried clumsily to seduce him.

"I want to give you a little kiss."

Rock grinned. "Where?"

"Where ever you want," she said in a sultry seductive voice. She tried to reach into his pants.

"Easy now, you're drunk and Scotty will be right back."

"Don't you want me?" She looked lustfully at him.

"Of course I do, but later."

"Okay." She ran her hands down his face, drawing his lips to hers for a light kiss.

"Did I tell you how sexy you are? I love your long hair, dark eyes, soft lips, strong hands."

She took his hand and kissed his fingers one by one. That was all the temptation he could take. Rock ran his hands over her back and pushed her harder on to his lap, grinding her down on him. Tongues dancing inside each other's mouths. For a moment. Jenna jumped up guiltily as Scotty walked back into the room. She stood and went inside the house, touching Scotty playfully on the arm as she left. Handing his friend a beer, Scotty sat across from Rock and looked at him.

"Do you really care for her or is this just a fling?"

"To be honest I'm not sure, she is so … sweet and naïve, I like her. But she's young but I'm not looking for a wife just yet."

Scotty sat back in the chair. "I just don't want Jenna's heart to get broken, she has a big one, and she's falling hard."

"I understand. She just has no idea what she's up against with the lawsuit and investigation. Missy's behind all this, you know."

Scotty agreed. "Yeah, I'm not sure why they ever hired her. She has no talent; she's been nothing but trouble since she came on the set."

"And a real whore, she'll do anyone," Rock said to Scotty.

Jenna stood in the doorway looking at the two men. Dropping the plate of desserts to the floor, she turned and ran down the stairs and out of the house.

Jenna's heart ached as the word stabbed her emotions and soul.

"Wait, Jen, we weren't talking about you," Scotty yelled as he went to the doorway.

"I'll handle this." Rock set his beer on a table and went after her. "Jenna, wait, damn it will you stop?" He crossed the highway to the beach and when he caught up with her, he grasped her wrist as she lumbered through the sand.

"It's true! I am nothing but trouble," she said as Jenna continued walking towards the ocean. Rock stopped her and pulled her to his chest as she sobbed. Holding her tight, he could do nothing but let her sob.

Finally, she stopped and sniffed.

Rock gave her a corner of his shirt to wipe her eyes. "We were talking about Missy, not you."

She blinked a few times, and then cried again. "Oh, Rock what am I going to do? I have no job, no car, no money. They want to sue me. I just don't know what to do. I have nothing."

"You have me, and you'll be fine, so don't worry." He held her to him.

"But what do we have really? A few nights of hot sex. I'm not even sure what you're looking for, if you are even looking for anything more that just a roll in the sheets." She turned away and looked out to the sunset.

Rock hugged her neck. "Let's just see what happens, I like you. You're sweet, sexy and you did save my life. That counts for something." He wrapped his massive arms around her chest, and pulled her down to the sand. They sat facing the sunset, his body behind hers.

"You have been through a lot the last few days, if you need some help dealing with all this I can call the doctor."

She shook her head. "I'll be fine."

Rock kissed the back of her neck. "Let's go back to the house."

"Alright, I'm still drunk you know."

"I know."

For the next week, Jenna hit the surf, cleaned Scotty's house and tried to refocus herself and get her life straightened out. Her insurance company gave a small settlement on her car. Nine hundred dollars? All those years of payments and I only got nine hundred bucks. Accepting the offer, she hoped she would get the check before her rent was due. I do need to get back to my apartment sometime, she thought and decided to see if Rock would take her there.

"Hello tiger, it's your love bunny. If you go to your place this weekend could you pick me up and drop me off at my apartment? Let me know if you can. I miss you, it's been like forever since I got to see you naked and put my lips on your ..." A loud beeping cut her off in mid sentence tell her she had ran her message to long.

On set, Rock listened to his voice mail in between takes. All daylong he yearned to hear from Jenna and he smile like a fool when her voice filled his ears. It turned to a scowl as Missy slithered up next to him.

"So now that what's her face is gone, maybe we should meet in your trailer later?" Missy tried her best to seduce him, rubbing her body against his.

"Let's keep things professional," he told her, taking her hands off his chest.

"You're going to regret it," she sneered as she walked away. Rock stood rolling his eyes. He left a message on Jenna's cell phone. "I'll be there at three this afternoon. Be ready."

Jenna clicked off after checking her messages, and then ran around packing all her belongings in preparation for her lover's arrival.

She found a pen and paper. "Scooter, thanks for everything, you're the best friend a girl could ever have. Love ya, Jenna."

She left the note on the kitchen counter and watched daytime television until she heard Rock's horn blowing. Running out of the house with her duffle bag, Jenna simply dropped it on the sidewalk the moment he put his arms out to her.

He missed the smell of her, the feel of her small body next to his. It seemed as if they had been away from each other for months even though it had only been five days. He put her bag in the rear seat, went around opening door for her, and they rode out of the beach city to the L.A. freeway north. On the way back to L.A. Rock told her all about the shoot and how the movie was soon to wrap production.

Jenna told him of her attempts to boogie board and cook. "And then a hammer head shark came and bit my head off," she said.

"Really, that's cool."

She shook her head. "You're not paying any attention to what I'm saying."

"What's that?" He glanced at her.

"Rock, are you okay?" Jenna frowned.

"Yeah, just tired."

"To tired to …?" she asked as she put her hand on his thigh and moved upwards.

"I swear I will pull this truck over right now if you don't stop." He winked.

"I wish you would, I've been so turned on for you for days! I am *sooo* frustrated." They both laughed.

"I know, Rock said, passing another car. "Laying bed alone was the hardest part. I tried not to think about it."

"You could have just taken care of it yourself," she told him.

"I was saving it all up for you." He said in a low tone.

Jenna grinned. "I can't wait." She grabbed his hand and kissed his knuckle as they exited the freeway into the One-o-one freeway. Traffic now crept along.

"So," he teased, "Scratch my back."

She pulled her legs under her body and leaned close to run her nails over his flesh.

"Lower, right there. Good. Thanks."

Jenna smiled. "You're welcome."

Pulling up in front of her building Rock decided to go into the apartment with her. They found a parking space on her street and she hung the permit sticker on his rear view mirror.

"So, you going to come…. in?"

"Absolutely. Who's that guy?" Rock said, nodding in the direction of her door.

"The apartment manager. What is he doing?" She did not give him time to answer before she jumped out of the truck and hurried to the door. Rock walked up behind her and read the large red letters. *EVICTION NOTICE.*

She was red with fury. "I am not late on my rent."

The foreign man sneered at her. "New owners are tearing down the building, Everyone's out."

Tearing down the bill, she read it aloud. "In ordinance with laws of emanate domain of the City of Los Angeles, you are hereby to abandon this residence in five days from posting of this decree."

Jenna was livid. "How am I supposed to find a place in LA in five days?"

Rock placed his chin on top of her head. "Nothing like been kicked while you're down." He felt her sigh heavily.

"You can stay with me," he offered.

"Thanks, but no thanks. I'll work something out; I can't take another hand out."

"I have plenty of room, besides I like having you around. As long you don't cook, we'll be fine."

She turned around and hit him with the paper playfully. He leaned over her and gave her his pay-attention-carefully look," If you don't open that door in the next five seconds I am going to take you in this hallway."

Jenna smiled and fumbled the keys as he placed his hands all over her.

"Race ya to get naked!" she yelled as she shut and locked the door.

Before she could get her top off he was naked and on her bed. Undressing in a hurry, she crawled on top of him.

"Oh how I have missed your big huge ..." Before she could finish he thrust inside her, sending a bolt of lightening crashing deep into her pink. She was riding him hard and fast he lavished the fact that she was doing all the work and he was inside his girl.

There was not doubt that she was his. He had to have her, keep her. No one had ever been able to make him come so hard or had gotten past the wall he put up around his heart. He sat up, Jenna still riding up and down on him. Their chests pressed together in a sweaty mesh of flesh. He could not get close enough to her. His arms reached under hers, forearms on her back, and hands on her shoulders pushing her down on his hard thick cock. Throwing her head back, Jenna came, shuttering at the forceful orgasm. Rock's volcano exploded deep inside her; and sent her into another powerful moment of ecstasy. He continued to plunge into her well after he came, the sensation was so intense he could not stop for a few minutes and the sensitive head of his penis touched soft folds deep inside her. They lay together holding each other tightly, overwhelmed by the passion of their lovemaking.

"God, I missed you," he told her, reaching over to the nightstand, picking up a photograph in a silver frame. "Who's this?"

"That's my best friend from high school. We were wild, we used to sneak into bars and drink and then get up and go to school the next morning. We had so much fun."

"Where is she now?"

Jenna rubbed his chest. "She went to college in Michigan. I haven't talked her in a while, so I am not sure."

"You never mentioned any family."

"No, I don't want to talk about them." She sighed.

"Understood. Let's go walk down to the Hamlet and get a burger."

They walked a block down from North Orchid to Hollywood Boulevard to a little restaurant. Holding hands as they crossed in front of the Hotel Roosevelt and walked over the marble stars, he stopped on Clark Gable, leaned her over as Rhett did to Scarlett, and gave her a Hollywood kiss. She giggled as he lifted her back up and a tourist stopped to watch them. After they were seated in the restaurant, Rock excused himself to talk with an older man dressed impeccably in what appeared to be a very expensive suit. Jenna watched the man greet Rock with sincerity. Both men watched Jenna as she smiled and asked the waiter for a beverage. Coming back to the table minutes later, Rock sat down and drank the dark beer she ordered for him.

"Who was that?" Jenna asked.

He set his drink on the table. "Head of the studio that I am doing my next movie for."

Jenna was interested. "Really. What kind of movie?"

"Sci-fi, futuristic. Filming in Canada." Rock sipped his beer again.

Jenna took a sip of her soda, and looked down at the menu thinking he would probably leave on a shoot and forget all about her.

"Don't worry, I'm not going to go off and forget about you."

Raising her head up, she smiled, "Mind reader."

The following morning they packed what they could in his truck—all her clothes, and shoes, throwing away her junky television, bed frame, mattress and two TV tray tables and her one lonely chair.

"Clothes, shoes and tax returns. My life in the back of a truck. Seems pretty simple and sad," she said to Rock as he unloaded the last of her things from the Escalade and into his garage.

"Any red stilettos in all those boxes?"

"I might have red."

"Grrr, baby Grrr!" Rock grinned.

Jenna stopped for a moment. "Rock, um, question."

He raised an eyebrow. "Yes?"

"What room am I going to be … um … sleeping in?"

"Why would you ask such a question?" Rock crossed his arms.

She blushed. "Well, I just wanted to know if I going to be a roommate or something more?"

He grabbed her in a rough embrace. "I want you in my bed every night, In fact I want you in it right now." He stooped down and lifted her over his shoulder and gave her a hard spank on the ass.

"Ouch, put me down you animal, sex maniac!" Jenna laughed and slapped at him.

He was not a bit apologetic. "You forgot man whore."

"Oh yeah." He said and took her into the house.

He threw her on the king size bed and stripped off his shirt, revealing his finely cut abs and chest. Jenna tingled inside. No one had ever made her feel like this. She trusted him completely, loved him, and wanted him.

"I want to please you."

He sat at the edge of the bed as Jenna knelt before him. Running her hands up his thighs into his shorts, he moaned at the touch of her hand on his growing penis. Lifting his ass, she pulled down the shorts, taking him in her mouth. The heat and wetness on him made his brain scramble. Watching her working on his pleasure heighten the sensuality and he nearly lost it as she looked up with her green-brown, I Dream of Jeannie eyes. Hard as stone he sucked air threw his teeth as she teased his head with her tongue. Tiny hands worked his shaft as she took him as far as she could without choking. Resting back on his elbows, Rock watched her for twenty minutes as she pleased him orally. What finally sent him over the edge was the deep guttural moaning and vibrations from her throat, bursting his hot liquid into her mouth. He lay back panting as she ran to the bathroom. Coming back to him, she laid on the bed over his chest, "Did I do right?" He was speechless and just put his hand on her hair.

Her head on his still heaving chest, Jenna twirled his hair in her fingers.

"I want you to know that I really care for you," he said.

"Promise me that if you ever are not happy with me staying, you will tell me. I do not want you to resent me or get angry. I have had enough of that to last me a lifetime."

"Alright, I will tell when you start to get annoying."

"Stop it, I'm serious!" she said as she threw a pillow at him. They lay for a half hour talking about nothing, as she massaged his scalp.

"Is this bothering you?" Jenna asked.

"No it feels good; I like how you touch me very much."

"Did your last girlfriend do this for you?" He knew where she was heading with this line of questioning.

"No, I usually get don't this involved; most women are looking for more than I am willing to give, and try to use sex to get it. I don't have much time for a relationship, so when women throw themselves at me, if I am in the mood I'll fuck them, then make them leave, or I get up and leave with an I'll call you."

Jenna could not believe how open he was being to her.

He continued, "Most women are looking for money, fame and will use any man to advance themselves."

"I'm not like that, I am going to make my way and work hard, make something of my self. I am going back to the University of Southern California … I dropped out to go to stunt school."

Rock nodded. "I know, Scotty told me the whole story."

"So you know I went to stunt school just to meet you after I saw you as that werewolf?"

"No, he didn't tell me that."

Embarrassment flushed her face. "Excuse me while I crawl under the bed."

Rock laughed. "I'm flattered, I think."

"I have one more confession to make since we are being so honest."

Hesitating he said, "Okay".

"I can't cook, Spaghetti is the only thing I know how to make, and apparently, I am not that good at it."

He laughed robustly. "I will take you out every night then. We'll go out tonight; we can hit the Lager House. Detroit's 60 Second Crush is playing tonight."

Jenna squealed. "That's the hottest rock club in L.A., it's like impossible to get in."

"We'll get in. I guarantee it."

He must have great connections, she thought.

"Wake me up at eight," he said before throwing a pillow over his head.

"Okay."

He drifted off to sleep as she stroked his back watching his strong features relax into a deep sleep. Since it was only one in the afternoon, and Jenna was not sleepy, she decided to unpack the boxes putting things away quietly as Rock slept. Man, I do have a lot of shoes, she thought as she stacked them carefully in the closet in the spare bedroom. After finishing around three, she slipped into the bed next to Rock and napped, waking up about seven-thirty.

I am going to get ready so he is not waiting on me, I know how men are, they do not like to wait on a woman. How would I know how men are? I have not had a boyfriend in two years. Oh well, I will start some coffee just in case. Jenna put on her sexy black leather pants she purchased from the Victoria's Secret catalog. That set her back a whole paycheck. A pair of matching spike heeled leather boots and the tightest zip front black shirt completed the outfit. Damn I look good, she thought.

"Yes, you do," Rock said.

"Reading my mind again?" She looked in the mirror at him standing behind her.

"I need to shower, bring me coffee."

She smiled and left to go get his cup. Coming back in and placing the mug on the nightstand, she closed the door behind her and went out to the kitchen and took a seat on the bar stool at the island. Flipping through a stunt magazine, Jenna could smell the Farhenheight cologne before he entered the room; her favorite men's cologne filled her senses. Rock grabbed his keys before walking to the door.

"Let's go."

Jenna walked to the truck, and waited for Rock to unlock the door. He stood at a covered automobile, next to the truck inside the garage.

"I wondered what was under here," Jenna mused.

Rock uncovered his brand-new Black Ferrari 350 spider.

Jenna screamed, "Holy moley! My favorite car! Can I drive it? Please? Please!? Please?"

"If you can tell what kind of engine it has, you can drive it," he tested her, not thinking she would have any clue.

"Three-fifty, two-twenty horsepower, dual twin cams, zero to sixty in four point five seconds."

He sighed, shook his head in defeat, and handed over the keys. Jumping in the driver's seat, Jenna carefully pulled it from the garage, and laid it on thick, jamming the gearshift into second.

When she he took curves at over sixty miles per hour and, Rock held onto the door handle and decided he had enough.

"Pull over!" he yelled.

"Sorry, I was drunk with speed and power," she joked. He snarled a bit as he got out and took over the driver's seat.

"I know the feeling," he said, zooming the rest of the way down the hill faster than she had driven, handling the car impeccably.

Jenna's stomach lurched as Rock pulled up to the front of Musso's, Jenna looked at him in shocked disbelief. How could he bring me here?

"You okay with going here?"

"Sure," she said, lying through her teeth.

"You'll be fine." He walked out, not holding the door for her.

She said climbing out of the Ferrari.

Socializing, Rock spoke to several acquaintances as Jenna sat alone at the table. Feeling uncomfortable sitting by herself, her thoughts of the night she was attacked replayed in her mind. Jenna held back tears as the manager came over to make his apologies for what happened the last time she was there. Rock returned, shook the manager's hand, and sat down next to her.

"Did they take action against Missy's assistant for the set up?" the manager asked Rock. Jenna's pain and shock registered on her face and Rock asked the manager to give them a minute. Her insides twisted as Rock tried to explain.

"I was going to tell you …," he said quickly.

Her voice was impassive. "I want to leave."

"Sure".

Rock had no idea how she would react that he held back this information from her. He hoped she would not flip out on him; he was not in the mood to deal with hysterical right now. He felt guilty enough for feeling this way, as she remained calm. He only reason he brought her here was because he heard Missy and her assistant were coming in as regulars and he wanted to the satisfaction of having them thrown out of his restaurant, another he secret he kept from her. The valet pulled the car to the curb, they got in, and Rock slowly inched away from the curb.

"Do you want to go home?" Rock asked.

"No, let's go to the club, we can talk about it later. Right now I need a drink."

In minutes, they were at another club. The valet rushed over, opening her door and helping her out.

"Look at the line," she said, worried that they would not get in.

He put his hand on the back of her neck possessively and led her directly thru the doors past the velvet ropes.

"You must know the owner," she wondered.

"I *am* the owner."

"Oh," she said coldly, feeling belittled and duped. Brushing his hand off of her neck, she followed him as he approached his private table. Rock parked a security guard next to her, left her alone and went off to meet greet his friends and check on his employees.

"I can't believe he just left me here with this goon standing over me. He takes me to the place I least wanted to be, keeps things from me, leaves me alone …"

Her train of thought was ground to a halt as she looked across the crowd, locking eyes with the most intensely mesmerizing, brooding guy she had ever seen. They both stared, each unable to turn away. Jenna smiled shyly, forgetting her pissy mood and anger at Rock. She turned away from his glare as someone called her name.

"What's so interesting?" Rock looked in the direction she had been staring.

"Nothing important. Kind of like I'm feeling right now," she said, cold and harsh, staring up at him from her chair. Rock sighed and rubbed the back of his neck.

"What do you want me to say?" he lamented.

"Why did I have to find out about the assistant and the guy in the alley from the manager of Musso's and not from you?" she said accusingly.

Rock stood, hand on hips staring at her, giving her an anger-filled stare.

"Look, I am not trying to start a fight, but you have to know that being caught off guard like that really pisses me off." she said, looking back at him with the same expression. Ten seconds passed before he made any type of movement at all.

Jenna stood up, prepared to leave. Rock looked down at the floor and back at her. Still not saying a word, he took hold of her elbow roughly and led her through the crowds, into the kitchen and into what seemed to be his office. He practically threw her in, and she turned around, leaning against the front of his desk. Slamming the door loudly, he placed an arm up, and propped it against the closed door. Jenna folded her arms, letting out a slight sigh, and stared at him, waiting for his response.

"I should have told you about Missy's assistant. I was wrong about that, is that what you wanted to hear?" he spilled out furiously.

"Why are you getting angry with me? What have I done?" she asked him. "You drove too fast, it's brand new!"

"What, this is about the Ferrari? Are you fucking kidding me?" she yelled.

Jenna glared at him with an indignant stare. Not getting any response from him, she went towards the door and reached for the handle. "I can not believe you would think that you not telling me about the assistant even compares to the Ferrari! Get out of my way." The pent up and suppressed anger started to surface inside both of them.

He grabbed her wrist tightly, but instinct kicked in and she blocked his other advancing hand. Trying again, she jumped aside, caught hold of his arm, and twisted it. Before she could even make her next move, he snatched both her wrists, swung her around, and pushed them up against the door over her head, shoving her against the door loudly.

Heart racing, breath shallow, temper flaring, she went to make her next move of dropping all her body weight and throwing a leg at his ankles taking him down to the floor. A move he had taught her. She executed perfectly, which took him by surprise when he went down to the floor, releasing her wrists to try to stop his fall.

Laughing aloud, she could not believe she got one over on him. Pissing him off royally, Rock could not believe she would do this to him, in his own office at his own club. Her fight instincts were no match for his, as he twisted his legs around her and prevented her from standing. With two quick movements, he was on top of her pinning her down the terrazzo floor. It felt just like the day they fought on set and he had her at his mercy pinned to the ground. Jenna struggle hard to break free, as Rock held her down tighter each time she wiggled.

"Let me go." She growled and writhed under him. Their eyes met in a furious stare and two souls crashed as passion exploded and they lunged for each other's lips. She grabbed the sides of his gorgeous face and held it in her hands as they locked lips and tongues. They rolled over the floor, lusting for each other passionately.

"Make love to me," he begged her and she tugged his shirt from his waistband.

Jenna pulled off her boots and struggled to get out of the leather pants as he pulled down his pants around his ankles, his military boots still laced up. He could not get inside her fast enough as his stone hard cock pulsated with anticipation.

He grabbed her waist and thrust himself inside her as they rolled over the tile. They moved from the floor, against the filing cabinet and finally bending her over the desk, he pulled back her hair as he placed his knee on the desk for traction and pounded her like a jack rabbit. Rock came so hard and fast inside her that he blacked out for a few seconds, collapsing on top her body that was sprawled over his desktop. Jenna was crushed by his weight and struggled for breath until he came out of his sex-induced coma. Rock pulled up his trousers, tucked in his shirt and suddenly the lock on the door opened, the sound of metal keys jingling. Oh my god, oh my god, she thought as the door opened. Jenna stood behind Rock but her panties and leather pants lay ten feet away. Embarrassment turned her pinker than she already was, and Jenna hoped that whoever opened the door could not see her nakedness, or her clothes lying on the floor. Hiding behind Rock's large frame, Jenna stood still, her exposed body crouched behind him, trying to conceal her nakedness.

"Ce faceti?" the strange voice said.

Jenna could not see who was talking but stood like a statue as the unidentified man talked to Rock while he held her behind him.

"Un moment, va rog," Rock told the man who was in fact, Rock's younger brother Christopher in the strange eastern European language, which shocked her that he spoke this unknown language. As the lock clicked, he turned around to her, pulling her naked bottom to him.

"You needed it that didn't you," she purred, putting her arms around his neck.

"Yes, so bad. Look, I didn't keep that from you on purpose; with everything that was going on I didn't think you needed any more stress." Rock explained.

"You should not have kept that from me and I am sorry, just being there brought up some bad feelings that I kind of haven't really dealt with and … I admit I was really jamming those gears on your car."

"My girl!" he told her, kissing her forehead.

"Me or the car? Should I be jealous of the Italian bird?"

"Who's in the bed and who's in the garage every night?"

Jenna just shook her head picked up her clothes and dressed. Before she could open the door, Rock stopped her, seizing her by the waist. Turning around and leaning back against the door, she waited.

"I need to tell you something."

Jenna cautiously looked up into his eyes.

He sighed, scratched at his head and swallowed.

"Rock, you … are you breaking up with me?"

"No, will you let me finish? I am trying to tell you that I never been happier. You … I can't lose you."

He pulled her to him and she tilted her head back so she could meet his eyes.

"The thought of disappointing you kills me, and I know I probably will again. God, you are so beautiful, how did I ever get so lucky?"

"I am the lucky one, you have been amazing to me, I got to meet my fantasy, and make it a reality. But, I feel like the one who will let you down. Sometimes I feel naive and helpless."

He cut her off. "You are far from helpless. Naive, maybe, I but I like that about you."

She closed her eyes as he leaned down, putting his cheek on hers.

"Tell me," he demanded and she knew exactly what he wanted to hear.

"I love you," she said.

"My girl. Let's go out and have drink."

"Are you ever going to say it to me?" she asked him.

"Don't I show you enough?"

Jenna shook her head. "I want to hear it."

Without answering, he placed his hands on her shoulders and led her out of the office. Slipping back out through the kitchen, they became part of the crowd, and went directly to the table.

"What do you want? Cranberry and vodka?" Rock yelled in her ear over the loud rock music.

Yelling back, Jenna told him. "I want you to tell me you love me."

Instead of telling her, he walked up to the bar and ordered from the mysterious man who stared at her earlier. She watched the bartender as he watched her and mixed the drink. Rock, who was leaning on the bar, turned around and winked. Jenna gave him a closed mouth smile. Rock returned his attention to the mystery hunk and picked up the drinks, bringing them over to her. As Rock walked back to the table, her eyes met the stud behind the bar again.

Mystery man stared from behind dark eyes. Pouring drinks without looking at the glasses, not taking his eyes off her, he watched as smile looked down and back to him. Jenna put her hand to her forehead, brushed her hair back behind her ear playfully, and looked up one more time to find him gone. Not even noticing the glass in front of her, Jenna put her hand down right into the drink.

"What's distracting you?"

"Oh, sorry, that guy was staring at me. The one behind the bar."

Rock held his glass up to his lips. "That's my brother, he's very moody. I would have introduced you when he came in the office but you were naked, and I would not was him to try to steal you away from me."

"Oh baby, no one could take me away from you," she said and cocked her head to the side, losing herself in Rock's dreamy brown eyes.

"Good, cause I would kill them," Rock said a little too seriously, picking up his scotch and sipping it. Rock's phone vibrated in his pocket and he took it out and excused himself to answer it in a quieter place. Jenna sipped her strong drink and coughed from the potent cocktail. Seeing her friend Elizabeth across the room, she grabbed her drink and fought her way across the crowd. The two greeted and hugged, hanging out and talking the rest of the night.

"Hey Jenna, how have you been I miss you in class."

"I know I dropped out to go to stunt school, I've been working, well up unto recently on Missy Manga's new movie."

"I can't stand that bitch, her song sucks, but I bet her acting does too."

Jenna snorted in disgust, "You don't know that half of it." So, she proceeded in great detail to tell Elizabeth the entire story start to finish.

Rock watched her from the bar, he was glad she spent the night talking to what appeared to be a good friend of hers. About to go over and tell her it was time to go, but he was distracted by one of the band members who came over to talk to him.

As the night wound down, the two girls said good-bye, Rock finished his drink on stage, talked to a few L.A. rockers and finally made his way over to her as she stood at the bar on the opposite side of the room.

"You've had enough," he told her in a fatherly way.

"Just water." She held out the straw for him to sip.

"Shit!" Rock said as a fistfight broke out between two drunken glam rockers, what looked like an Axl Rose impersonator and his posse. Rock, several bar tenders and one large bouncer pulled apart the catfighters, who were shouting insults about each others lack of style and getting in one last dig, the Axl Rose wanna-be picked up a beer bottle and hurled it, missing his target and sending it directly towards Jenna's head. The brown bottle flew across the bar directly at her face. At the very last second, Jenna noticed it. Closing her eyes preparing for the hit, she cringed. Confused when no impact happened, she opened her eyes slowly to see Rock's brother, Christopher's huge strong tattooed arm, bottle in his fist centimeters from her face. His stare was emotionless, blocked by the dark sunglasses that concealed his eyes. He lowered the bottle as Jenna looked up at him.

"You stopped it," Jenna said to him in amazement as Rock approached his brother and gave him a death stare. His brother walked away, looking over his shoulder at Jenna who watched his every move.

"You alright?" Rock asked.

"I'm fine; your brother—he stopped the bottle. It was heading right towards my face. He snatched it in mid-air!"

"We're going home," Rock said, dragging her off the barstool. Rock grabbed her by the scruff of the neck and led her quickly away. Glancing over her shoulder, Jenna looked back at Rock's brother and gave him a quick smile, but he did not smile back, just lifted his head in acknowledgement as she mouthed thank you to him. Rock's brother continued to look intently until she left the club.

In late summer, they had been together for six weeks. Signing up for classes at the University of Southern California, made Jenna feel excited about earning a degree. Jenna went full time, studying hard in finance and business classes. Both her and Rock were glad to have put all danger and drama behind them as the whole incident on set was swept under the rug by the studio. Jenna had received a small settlement from the studio that she used to pay for her college tuition.

One morning Jenna was up early and out the door, leaving Rock a note. *Had to catch the early bus. I want to study before class. Be home around six. Love you, Jen.* Something crinkled and scratched his face. Rock swatted at it and blinked to clear his vision. He smiled as he read the note before getting out of bed to start his day. He worked out, returned some business calls, and dialed Scotty.

"What's the rundown?" Rock asked his friend.

"I need you back on set for a few days, some re-shoots. Why don't you and Jen come down to the beach for a few days?"

"I think Jenna's in class every day, but maybe on the weekend we'll have time."

Scotty said he hoped so. "Cool, see you Wednesday, ten in the morning."

Rock hung up and took the Ferrari rolling to his club to check on the new sound system he was installing. After working at the club until the early evening, Rock came home to find the house empty.

"It's six-thirty, where the hell is she?" he barked. In a pissy mood, he tried to call her cell phone and it went directly to her voice mail.

Rock left a terse message. "I thought you would be home by now; call me as soon as you get this message." He wanted to see her, they had been spending so much time apart; he had had a stressful day and just wanted to feel her next to him. The later it got the angrier he became. Was she out with her friends? Was she seeing someone else? His mind raced and he was ready for a fight.

The time was nearly nine before she walked in. As soon as he heard the door, he charged out.

"Where have you been? I have been sitting here worrying all night. I called you, but you don't bother to return my call?"

Jenna set her bag on the foyer table. "I'm sorry, my cell phone battery died. I missed my connector bus. So I …"

"So you walked? All the way from Sunset?" he questioned her.

She nodded wearily. He lifted the bag from the table. "This weighs a ton." His voice softened.

"I had five classes today. I really have to go study; I have an exam tomorrow."

He looked at her drawn face. "Did you even eat anything today?"

"No, I didn't have any money," she said.

"Why didn't you ask me?" he asked, his tone rising again.

"I hate to ask you, I have to do this on my own. I do not want a hand out. Look, please, we have been over this before and I do not want to start an argument. I need my energy, I have to study." She glanced up with sad puppy dog eyes, making his heart melt.

"Go study, I'll bring you something to eat," he said backing down.

She took the book bag into the spare bedroom, sat down at the desk, and opened he books.

"I made you a sandwich … Jen?" He walked around to the chair to see her head to her chin, sleeping with pen in hand. She has been working so hard, he thought, as he lifted her out of the chair and laid her on the bed. She slept like angel as he sat next to her, running his hands over her forehead. I never expected this, I was not looking for anyone, and there you were. She completes my heart and I love having her here, he thought to himself. Leaving her sleeping, he knew what he wanted to do, and walking out to the living room, he grabbed his phone to make it happen.

Waking in a panic, Jenna jumped from the bed and ran out to the living room to find the time. Sick to her stomach that she overslept, Jenna found Rock sitting at the kitchen table in his boxers reading the morning paper and drinking his coffee.

"What time is it? I'm late," she asked in a panic running, around the house.

"What time is your exam?" he asked coolly.

"Ten o'clock!"

"It's eight-thirty."

"I'm going to miss my bus," Jenna said as she ran back into the spare bedroom to pack her books. Rock laughed aloud and was pleased when she ran back quickly and kissed him.

"Good Morning, I love you, I have to go." Planting another kiss on him, she missed his lips and got his chin instead. Running towards the door, she flung it open and stopped dead in her tracks. He stood behind her in the doorway, watching her reaction. Dropping her backpack, Jenna screeched like a hoot owl.

"Is this … did you … how …?"

Before her, draped with a large red bow, was a brand new shiny, black Volkswagen Jetta. Custom wheels, sunroof, and a cool scoop on the back made the car look like he had it customized just for her. She looked at him as he threw the keys at her and she caught them with one hand over her head.

"You're not going to be late today."

Running to him, Jenna jumped up into his arms wrapping her legs around his waist, kissing all over his face.

"I can't believe this! Thank you, oh my god, I love you," she said as she hugged him so tight he had to pry her arms from around his neck so he could breathe. "Oh Rock, I can't accept this, it's too much. How can I every repay you?"

"You can start by getting to class and passing your exam."

Jenna kissed him passionately, and he set her down, walked over to the car and opened the door for her. Sniffing in that new car smell, Jenna ran her fingers over all the buttons and gadgets.

"I love it, it exactly what I wanted. How did you know? I don't care how you knew, oh my god Rock, I can't believe you!"

"Call me later and we can arrange a little celebration," he said throwing her backpack into the back seat.

Zooming down the hill, the new car handled like a dream as she sped towards the campus. Arriving with enough time to get a few study moments in, Jenna aced her exam and went to her other classes, but all she thought about was how wonderful Rock was and ways to thank him.

Another month later, Jenna started working for Scotty at the Stunt School, running the office and putting her schooling to good use. Calling in to the school from a movie location in San Diego, Scotty asked Jenna how everything was going.

"Great I'm done with classes. I don't go back until August third, so I can work full-time until then."

"Good, come to the beach this weekend, I miss you and Rock. Let's have a cold beer."

Jenna smiled. "How can I resist? I will ask Rock, I'm not sure what his schedule is. He's on the shoot up in Ventura."

"Call me later, I have to get back to work, oh and have the gun class moved back to Tuesday."

"I will do, bye Scotty."

Spending the evening shopping at the Beverly Center, Jenna purchased a new sheer nightie. Rock will like this, she thought with devilish intent. Getting home she unpacked the groceries and the new sexy lingerie and thought, where the hell is he? Jenna gave up on the lingerie, put on one of his t-shirts and fell asleep waiting for him. At nearly three, Jenna awoke to a quiet house and an empty bed. Sitting up, she heard strange voices arguing. Sleepily she strolled out to the living room to find Rock standing in the doorway yelling in the eastern European language she did not understand. The words flowed angrily to the unknown shadow of a man outside the door.

"What's going on?" she asked him, yawning.

"Go back to bed!" he growled at her.

"But—."

"Damn it, do as I tell you!" he screamed out violently.

Slinking back like a wounded animal, Jenna retreated quickly into the bedroom but not before she got a glimpse of the firearm he was holding and the blood spattered all over his hand as well as his arm. Confused and scared, Jenna sank down into the covers as the shouting grew louder, more intense. What is going on? She thought as she heard the last few shouts in the unknown tongue.

When the door slammed her heart leaped out of her chest, and she jumped out of the bed to go check on Rock. Standing in the doorway, she watched him drinking straight from the bottle of whiskey. Pacing across the living room drinking chug after chug, his face flushed with pure rage and in his anger, he threw the bottle at the fireplace. In the angry state, his aim was off and the bottle missed its target and shattered barely a foot from her head. Pieces of glass from the bottle flew all over her and she let out a loud shriek.

Until she cried out, he had no idea she was there.

"Damn it," he cursed as she ran back into the bedroom.

His long legs carried him into the bedroom in time to see her duck into the bathroom to get away from his rage. He caught her arm as she stepped into the bathroom, and pulled her out into the bedroom. Unaware of his strength, he squeezed her arm so tight it she gasped.

"I didn't hear anything, I swear," she pleaded. "Please let me go."

His demeanor grew darker, and he ignored her pleas.

"You and I were together all night, right?" Rock said adamantly giving her a hard tug. "We were?" she asked.

"It wasn't a question. If anyone asks and I were here all night, got it?" he said as he took hold of her other arm and shook her.

"Yes, all night. Please let go, you're hurting me."

Releasing her, Rock took the bloody gun, slammed it down on the dresser top, and went into the bathroom. Standing frozen in shock, Jenna did not move until the noise of the shower running jolted her back to reality. Slipping back into the bed, she clutched at the pillow, trying to make sense out of what had just happened.

Ten minutes later, Rock came out, a towel wrapped around his waist and he dropped it before he lay down next to her. Rolling over to the edge away from him, soft tears fell from her eyes. She wiped them away not wanting him to know she was crying, but he knew she was and reached out for her. Part of him wanted to take out his frustration on her sexually, part of him wanted to beg her forgiveness, but he did not do either.

Feeling like shit for treating her like that, he lay staring at the ceiling and blew out all the air in his lung in exasperation. For twenty minutes, he contemplated the right words to say to her to make it right.

"I didn't know you were standing there," he finally spoke. Rolling over on his side, he looked over her to find she had cried herself to sleep. His stomach turned sour as he saw the marks he had left on her arms. Watching the expression on her sleeping face made him even more upset as he saw the wrinkled brow and he knew the nightmares had begun.

She tossed and cried out from her slumber, "No, stop, no ..."

Torture squeezed his head, the stress tap danced on his skull as he felt like an ass for treating the love of his life this way and seeing she was going through now with tormented nightmares. This was one part of his life he never wanted to share with her, expose her to, and defiantly not involve her in but it was too late. Rock was born Constantine Contros, a Romanian noble, he came from a long line of warriors, knights, thieves, mastermind criminals, gangsters and killers. Cursing himself in his mind, he did the one thing he never wanted to, show her this side of his past life. Getting up, he sat on the edge of the bed and placed his head in his hands.

The next morning he was gone. Waking up alone was the worst. For three torturous days, Jenna waited, not hearing from him at all. On pins and needles, she went through the motions of the day, going to class, eating alone, sleeping alone. She had no idea where he was or when he would return and why would he leave his own house and not just kick her out. On the fourth day, Jenna jumped up off the couch after hearing a car door slam from out in the drive. Flinging the door open, Jenna was taken aback as two gold badges flashed in her face.

"Can I help you?" she asked the men.

"We're looking for Constantine. Is he here?" the detective asked as he peered past her into the house.

"No, what is this about?"

"Madam, we ask the questions," he snapped.

"Who are you?" the detective grilled her.

"Who are you?" she retorted.

"L.A.P.D. So you said you did not know where he is?"

Jenna shook her head firmly. "No, I answered you when you asked if he was home. He's at work."

"Was he working on Sunday night?

She stared. "No, we were home all night. Why?"

"He didn't say, leave in the middle of the night for some reason?" The detective stared too.

"I told you we were here all night, so if you do not mind I have an exam to study for," she said trying to shut the door, but the detective's foot prevented it.

"When Constantine returns, tell him we want to speak to him." He shoved a card at her face. Jenna snatched the card out of the detective's hand shut the door and locked it. Nausea flooded her stomach as she realized she just lied to the police. Practically running to the phone, she fumbled with the numbers as she called Rock's cell phone. Three rings led to his voicemail. "Rock," she said shakily, but tried to calm her voice.

"Rock, the police were here looking for you … can you please come home? I'm sorry I made you mad, please call me, I miss you."

Hanging up, Jenna sat and waited in vain for his return call. Hours passed into the night. She sat outside on the patio watching the stars in the navy sky.

In the dark of the night, a shape moved in her peripheral vision sending her to her feet. Out of the shadows, Rock stepped towards her, wearing an emotionless face.

Not sure how to react, she stood like a statue before him, staring directly into his dark brown eyes. Jenna scanned his face, unsure if he was going to kiss her or hit her. His eyes moved from her face to her arms, searching the fading bruises on her biceps that were compliments of his anger, then looked back up to her face.

Disappointment filled her eyes, and since he was not speaking, Jenna turned and went back into the house into the bedroom. Walking in to the room, she could see the anger rising in his face in the mirror over the dresser as he found her packing her things. Placing the already packed suitcase on the floor, Jenna turned towards the closet to retrieve the rest of her belongings. Picking up the suitcase, Rock pitched it across the room, smashing the case into the wall and sending clothing all over the floor.

"Packing? Were you just going to leave with out telling me?" he fumed.

"Just taking after you," she said back. "You abandoned me."

He raised his backhand to her, but the sight of her flinching in expectation made him draw back and lower his arm.

"I'm sorry … oh god, Jenna, please." He fell to his knees and grabbed her around waist placing his face on her womb.

"Don't leave, forgive me, I need you with me," he begged as tears fell from his eyes.

"Tell me …" she whispered. He wanted to but could not get the words out.

She cupped his face in her hands and bent over to kiss his lips. "I love you, but I can not be, will not be treated like that again. Everyone I truly loved has abused me in past I and I won't go through it again. I deserve better."

"Oh Jenna, you're right, I was wrong, I can't live with out you, you mean more to me than anyone ever has, please don't go."

She combed his hair with her fingers. "I'm here, and I want to make you happy, I don't know what I did to make you so angry to leave but I am sorry."

"No, no it's not you, it was all me. You did not do anything, it is all my fault. I rarely let anyone in, and now you own my heart."

"I lied to the police." she was not sure why she blurted it out, it just slipped.

His demeanor changed, "What did you tell them?"

"That you and I were here all night."

"Good."

"Are you going to tell me what's going on?"

"It's best if you don't know." He told her coldly.

She sat on the edge of the bed, looking down at the floor. He pushed her back and proceeded to kiss her, running his hands over her body.

"Rock, we need to talk."

Unable to hear her over the rushing of blood in his ears, he pulled at the sleep boxers she was wearing.

"Rock, please." Jenna gave in anyway as he continued to release himself from his pants and brought her down to the mattress.

"I missed being in you," he said as he ejaculated with force inside her.

"Rock?" she said as he rolled off her.

"Yes." He said out of breath from the quick hot sex.

"Promise you will never leave me."

"I promise." He said and fell asleep.

Cruising down to Hollywood Blvd. the following morning, Jenna stopped at Starbucks for an iced green tea, specialty coffee for her lover and over-priced bagels. Parking at the curb, Jenna ran in, ordered, and proceeded out the door. To her left was the newsstand filled with papers and magazines, and the headline of the latest tabloid mad stopped her in her tracks.

'Assistant to Hollywood Actress Found Murdered.'

Tearing open the paper, Jenna's eye widened; Missy Manga's picture was splashed all over the pages. Throwing a five-dollar bill at the attendant, Jenna jumped in her VW and raced back up the hill. An unfamiliar car sat in her driveway. Shoving the paper quickly into her purse, she hurried with the hot cups of coffee back into Rock's home.

"What's going on?" she asked and set down the paper mugs.

The two detectives and Rock turned to look at her as she stepped into the foyer.

"Mrs. Constantine, are you still standing by the story that your husband was home all evening on Sunday?"

"First of all, I am not his wife, second, I told you there is no story, and we were home all night, having amazing sex, if you need to know what we were doing."

"That's what your husband—I mean boyfriend said," one detective offered. He closed up his notebook. "Thanks for your time. Don't plan on leaving the country anytime soon. We'll be in touch."

Rock closed the door and spun when Jenna's asked him, "Have you seen this?" She shoved the paper into his face, opening the page with the murder story.

"What of it?" he sneered with obvious agitation.

"The other night? Me covering for you? The gun and the blood, all the hell she put … caused. Did you …?" Before she could ask if Rock had killed the assistant, he backhanded her face so hard that she saw stars. The blow sent her down to the floor and Jenna landed on her hands and knees. Reaching up to her face, Jenna touched her left cheek which stung like a sunburn.

Rock pulled her up to her feet. "How dare you accuse me, in my own house!" he said and threw her back down to the floor.

"Don't you *ever* hit me again!" She screamed at him as he followed her to the door. Rock yelled at her to get back in the house but she had grabbed her keys and purse, and headed directly towards her car still holding her face. She jumped in and zoomed away down the hill double the speed limit. Unknowing to Rock or Jenna, the two detectives sat watching from across the street.

I can not believe he did that. How could he? Oh my god, did her really kill Missy's assistant? Jenna pondered a million thoughts as she sat, caught in a traffic jam the on the four-lane freeway. Finally, traffic moved and she exited at Springdale Avenue in Huntington Beach. Jenna took the street down to the pacific coast highway and turned left to Scotty's.

As the car slowed to the curb, she found Scotty putting out the garbage.

"What are you doing here?" he asked, approaching the car.

"I didn't know where else to go," Jenna said unsteadily.

"What happened to your face?" he asked, turning her cheek with his hand.

"Rock and I had a fight."

"And …?" he said as she started to cry. He helped her out of the car and held her to his chest.

"And I asked him if … I … He hit me."

Scotty held her at arms length and peered closely at her face. "He hit you?"

"Oh, Scotty, I don't know what to do. I love him, but he scares me sometimes. Strange thing have been happening with him. I came in and the police were there and I just read about the murder in the paper."

Scotty frowned in confusion. "Wait, what murder?"

"Missy's assistant was found shot in Los Feliz. And Rock had a gun and there was blood and he yelled at me and threw a bottle at me." Jenna began to hyperventilate as she told him.

"Calm down. When did he throw a bottle at you?" He asked her sternly as he took hold of her shoulders again.

"The other night, Sunday night, he was arguing with someone in the middle of the night. I couldn't see who it was ... I couldn't understand the language; he yelled at me to go back to bed and when the shouting had stopped, I came out of bedroom and he smashed a liquor bottle next to my head." Jenna took a deep breath and continued. "Then he left, disappeared for days, until yesterday. When I asked him about everything—that's went he backhanded me. So, can I stay here tonight?"

"No, sorry honey, but I have company coming over. Go home and talk to him, okay?" Scotty shook his head.

Jenna pleaded, "I can't go back there, Scotty, I'm afraid."

He was adamant. "Listen to me, I'll talk to him. Everything will be fine. He won't do it again. I promise."

Jenna was shocked that he turned her away but decided to listen to him. She thought long and hard as she drove around Southern California for hours. No one deserves to be treated like this. How can he say he loves and then hit me? Someday I promise to help girls who get hit, she thought. Leaving Scotty's house she felt more confused at his turning her away then at Rock's odd behavior. The tears started just as she stopped at the first red light she came to. Pulling the car into the first business she came to she just sat in the parking lot for a while to try to make sense of what was going on. She had no place to go, begrudgingly she headed back to Rock's house.

"She on her way home. Deal with her without hitting this time or you will have me to deal with and trust me I make good on my word." Scotty snapped at Rock's voice mail, clicked off the phone and walked back into the house.

Pulling up to the house, Jenna's hands shook as she turned off the ignition. She stepped carefully into the living room and noticed right away a huge bouquet of pink iris and yellow tiger lilies that sat on the coffee table. Jenna sniffed the flowers as she took out a card that read, 'I'm Sorry.' Touching the soft velvety petals, she forgot about her stinging cheek and Rock's harsh words. Behind her, Jenna felt the heat of his towering body and she backed up to him.

"They're beautiful, thank you."

His voice was tired. "I lost control. It won't happen again. Okay?"

She nodded her head as she leaned against him.

Turning her around to face him, he put his strong hand gently under her chin and lifted her face to meet his eyes.

"Tell me," he demanded softly.

"Love you."

"Good girl."

Why can't I resist him? His very words melted her, even as he leaned in and placed a slow kiss on her lips.

Jenna moved her head out of his reach. "Rock, you know I would do anything for you, right?"

"You will," he began.

She touched his chest. "I would. I have never been in love like this, you are my everything and I want to make you happy. I was not testing you, I just wanted to know. I will stand by you even if you were maimed, broke, and couldn't get it up."

He laughed, "No problem there. Speaking of which, I have a surprise for you. It's in the bedroom."

Jenna looked at him trying to figure out what he meant. Walking in the room, she found on the bed a black beaded corset, French lace panties, patent leather thigh high boots and what appeared to be some kind of black leather dog collar.

"You want me to wear this?" She frowned, backing away.

He stared at her. "Put it on."

Jenna opened her mouth to protest and he cut her off. "Don't question, just do." She looked at him with an untrusting glance, scooped up the outfit and went into the bathroom.

"Well if he wants kinky, he's going to get it." She took her time putting on smoky eyeliner, dark red lips, and pulled her hair back into tight chiffon. Placing the collar around he neck, Jenna looked in the mirror one last time, took a deep breath, and went into vixen mode.

Strutting out to him, she watched as his eyes nearly popped out of the sockets. She approached the bed slowly.

"Oh, baby," he said lustfully, he wanted her to be able to feel she was in control and thought this way she could be regain some power over him.

"Did I say you could speak? Get off that bed and come here." The commanding tone excited him and he went to her. "On your knees, slave."

Rock was not sure where this was coming from, from shrinking violet to dominatrix, he liked her demanding him and obeyed willingly.

"Lick my boots." He looked at her hesitating, and she shoved his head down.

"Now!" she yelled out. He bent down and obeyed. Taking the tip of the pointed toe boot, Jenna placed it under his chin, lifted his head to make him look at her.

Removing the tip from his chin, she placed the spike heel on his shoulder, digging the heel into his collarbone on purpose and hoped it hurt as much as the slap he gave her. It hurt like a son of a bitch and he grabbed her ankle tight and lifted the boot over his shoulder. The leather creaked loudly in his ear as he ran his hand over her smooth thigh. Clutching the hair on the back of his head, Jenna pulled his face closer to feel his hot breath over the lace panties.

"Lick me," she demanded. With one strong motion, he tore the fabric from her body and covered his mouth over her. He moaned as pushed him deeper into her. Throbbing waves crashed inside her as she came hard from his tongue-lashing.

Taking her leg off his shoulder, she barked out orders at him.

"Take off you pants ... Get on the bed ... Lay on your back."

Damn, I wish I had a whip, she thought. Lying there, his erection grew to full attention as she crawled up his legs, leather rubbing against his tight thighs. He closed his eyes as she stopped at sat over his hips. The heat of her folds beckoned his manhood to her.

With one of her small hands, she pulled his giant cock inside her, and slid down over him. He placed his hands on the outside of her moving hips helping the motion of way she was riding him. She did not want this; she wanted to control every move. Want him to let her dominate. Taking his hands she held his wrists in front of her, she used them as leverage to lift her up and down as she rode him into a vigorous rhythm. It did not take along before he came so forcefully that she could feel it shooting inside her.

He laid with his arm over his forehead as she slipped off him and went into the bathroom, washed the make up off, undressed, and put on his t-shirt returning as his fresh face girlfriend. Rock wrapped his strong arms around her.

"Sorry I got angry."

"Hit me again I will leave and never come back." She looked him straight in the eyes.

"It won't happen again," he promised. Jenna smiled, damn right it won't.

"Look what we got in the mail," she called to him as he poked his head out of the back of the truck he was loading some equipment into.

"What's that kiddo?" Rock smiled at her.

Jen held the envelope for him to see. "An invitation to the premier and after party!"

He took it from her. "Where?"

"Mann's Chinese Theatre." She nearly swooned and stole the invitation back from him. "I need a dress."

He caught the back of her shorts as she was walking away and pulled her back to him as she was reading the invite. Nuzzling her behind her ear, he said, "You can have any dress you want. Shoes and purse too."

She raised an eyebrow. "Oh yeah, what's that going to cost me?"

He winked. "Two nights of being my love slave."

"I'm that every night, master," she teased.

"Here." He pulled out the black American Express card. "Buy anything you desire."

As Jenna reached for the credit card, he pulled back, teasing her. "Kiss first."

On her tiptoes, she kissed him and swiped the card from his hand. "Love you!" Racing out to her car, Jenna sped down the hill nearly taking out some tourists who had stopped to take a picture of the Hollywood sign on Beachwood Drive. *Beverly Center first, then Melrose, maybe Rodeo. He said get what ever I want.*

Parking in the public parking lot, she spotted a high-end boutique that she had always wanted to go into but never had the opportunity or the balls to. After an hour browsing the racks, Jenna found the perfect dress. Holding up the short mini with a lace over cover, she held it against her and looked into the mirror.

"What exactly are you looking for?" A sales clerk sniffed and looked down her nose at Jenna.

She bristled. "I'd like to try this on."

"It's very expensive. If you can not afford such an item, I suggest not even trying it on." The clerk smiled thinly.

"Are you serious? I can afford any thing in this store," Jenna retorted in the same tone.

The clerk was not impressed. "Anyone with a stolen credit card can claim that."

Jenna placed the dress back on the rack slowly and held her head high as she stared at the bitchy clerk and walked out. Missy Manga stepped out of the fitting room and handed the clerk a hundred dollar bill.

Jenna did everything she could to hold back tears until she was in her car. Fishing for her sunglasses, she slipped them on as the tears spilled out from the corners of her eyes. The experience crushed her; she forgot shopping and went back to the house where she curled up on the couch. Coming from the kitchen, Rock looked puzzled.

"I thought you would be shopping all day. Did you find a dress that fast?"

"Here." She handed the credit card back to him. "The clerk wouldn't sell me a dress; she said the only way I could afford it was if I had a stolen card."

The look of sadness and embarrassment made his heart break. "Screw those pretentious bitches; you *can* afford the whole store."

"I'm not going to the premier. I'm probably not welcome anyway and it's true—the sales lady took one look at me and knew I had to have some one else's money. I'm nobody." She turned her face away to prevent him from seeing the tears streaming down her cheeks.

He sat down next to her and pulled her face in his direction. "You are not a nobody. You are my girl—smart, beautiful and loving. One person's words cannot change who you are or what you will become. Now dry your tears, we have to buy a dress." He pulled her off the sofa.

"You're the best." She launched into his body and kissed him.

So, he said as he drove down Rodeo drive. "Which store was it?" Jenna pointed to the high-end Italian designer shop.

"Wait here." He parked the sleek Ferrari right in front of the store.

Spying him, the clerk scrambled to get to Rock, knowing how much he spent each time he was in there and how much commission she made.

"Welcome back Mr. Constantine; how can we be of assistance?"

He stood at the register. "I'd like to know who waited on my girlfriend this morning."

The clerk tilted her head. "What did she purchase?"

"Nothing. She left empty handed because someone called her a thief."

Upon hearing his tone, the manager approached. "Good afternoon, Mr. Constantine. What seems to be the problem?"

He frowned. "I sent my girlfriend in here and your clerk told her she could not buy a dress because she probably had a stolen credit card."

"Is this true?" the manager asked the clerk.

The clerk was not apologetic. "She looked like she couldn't afford it. We have those kinds in here all the time!"

"My apologies, Rock—Mr. Constantine." She turned to the red-faced clerk. "Get your things; you're terminated."

"Whatever!" the bitchy clerk said as she walked to the counter, grabbed her purse, yanked the dress Jenna had picked up and threw down on the floor in a last ditch bitch move, and stormed out to where Jenna sat in the Ferrari waving to her.

"Sorry, Rock, I had no idea what happened. So …, you have a girlfriend now, does that mean you won't be calling for late night fun anymore?" the manager teased.

"It's serious."

She batted her eyelashes. "Well, I would like to meet the woman who captured the sexiest playboy in L.A., but if it doesn't work out …"

"You'll be my first call." He winked at the manager and walked out.

By the time they finished shopping both were exhausted and had no luck in finding a dress, but returned with the trunk full of shoes, purses, and makeup. However, when they arrived at home there was a white box wrapped in pink ribbon on their front doorstep. Jenna ran to it and pulled out the small white card. *Sincere apologies, hope you enjoy it.* Inside was the dress Jenna wanted to try on.

"Oh Rock, it the dress!" Jenna gushed and rushed into the bedroom to try it on. "Perfect fit."

He appeared in the doorway. "Let me see."

"No, not till the premiere." She took it off, packed it in the box, stuffed it in the closet, and rejoined her handsome lover. "So, what are we going to do tonight?'

He dropped onto the sofa. "I have to be at the club; we have a great band playing. Want to go?"

She smiled. "Can I wear my patent leather boots?"

"Absolutely not, till later, but the collar is okay," he teased.

"I think you should wear the collar, so I can keep a tight leash on you. All those women throwing themselves at you all the time; I might get jealous."

He tweaked her nose. "I hope so."

Arriving to the club around eleven, they found a building packed to the walls with rockers and actors tripping to the band. He led her in, aware that men stopped dead in their tracks to gawk at her in the slinky, backless lilac chain-mail top and tight leather mini skirt. Jenna didn't notice them staring. They were seated quickly at Rock's private table. She turned to him. "How long have you owned this place?"

He stood. "A few years. I have to go back in the office and check on things. I'll be back, order whatever you want."

"Thank you lover."

Kissing the top of her head, Rock pulled her hair before walking to the back to his office. Instead of staying seated, she strutted over to the bar. Jenna looked around, trying to get the bartenders attention.

"Jenna, Jenna!" A voice came from behind her.

Her classmate and friend from college was there to celebrate her birthday. Elizabeth pushed past a crowd of large rockers to get to her. Ordering a bottle of Rock's most expensive champagne, Jenna took her friend back to Rock's table. One of Rock's barmaids came over with the bucket of opened bubbly and two glasses. They toasted to birthdays, no classes, and new friendships.

"Let's dance," her friend said, dragging Jenna to the dance floor.

"Oh yeah!" Jenna said as they left the table and joined with more girls for the birthday celebration. As the other girls danced and grinded on each other, Jenna looked over her shoulder to see Rock's younger brother watching her intensely. He stood at the side of the stage, watching her and her only. The gorgeous features of his face were striking and mysterious. His head was covered by a black bandana holding back what looked like naturally dark hair like his brother. Burning through her, his stare made her feel self-conscience but flattered. There was something about the way his eyes bore into her that made her sweat in her naughty parts and she had not idea why.

As the song ended, she went back to the table, leaving the dance floor and her friend behind. Looking back as she walked she did not see Rock's brother watching her anymore. Rock met her carrying another bottle of bubbly.

"Where did all your friends go? I liked the way you were dancing."

She waved her hand. "They're still on the dance floor. I just needed a drink."

"I need a kiss," he whispered in her ear.

"Where?" she purred back teasingly. Without hesitation, her took her hand and led her swiftly to his back office.

Jenna giggled in anticipation. "What are you up to, Mr. Constantine?"

They made their way through the kitchen quickly and the cook stood out of the way. The whole kitchen staff stared; all of them knew what was going down. He shut the door, walked around to his desk, took a seat, and tried to pull her down on his lap.

Jenna stopped him. "Oh no, you said you wanted a kiss and I want to give it to you someplace special."

Oh yeah, he thought as she knelt before him and worked on the zipper of the black leather pants he wore. Springing to solid as soon as she put her soft hands on his manhood, he slid down the seat a bit to get comfortable as she took him in her hot little mouth circled her tongue over his head. Watching her devour him with a voracious pace, he moaned in delight as she growled her throat sending vibrations over the sensitive foreskin. She went on pleasing him, and almost to the point of losing his load, she flicked her sultry eyes up at him and he closed his eyes ready to explode and did, filling her mouth.

Keys rattled in the door. Rocks quickly straightened in his chair, making Jenna bang the back of her head on the desk drawer. He pushed her further under the desk. Good thing you can't see under the desk from the front, they both thought at the same time.

"Ce faceti?" Rock's brother asked.

Below the desk, Jenna did not know who spoke to Rock. The footsteps came closer to the desk as Jenna froze, still holding onto his sinking erection. She swallowed hard, trying to be quiet as a church mouse, but started to gag.

"Nothing, I'll be out in a minute." Rock told him in English.

"Scuzati-ma," the voice said and then she heard the sound of the door closing behind him.

"That was close!" a little voice said from under the desk.

"Let's get back out there," he said as he zipped up his trousers. Jenna climbed out from under the desk and fixed her face in the mirror. He went to open the door and Jenna stopped him.

"Kiss my neck first."

He obliged with a smooch and a firm hands on her ass.

"Who's your girl?" she asked him.

"You are."

"Where are my friends?" she said aloud. The gang of chicks whooped as she came back to the dance floor and they all danced and flirted and drank excessively till closing time.

"They left me, it's my birthday, and those bitches left me here," a drunken Elizabeth told Jenna. Half in the bag herself, Jenna agreed.

"Those tramps, I'll drive you home in my Jetta, oh wait I didn't drive, good think, thing cause I is dee-drunk." Her voice was thick and slurred. The two laughed as Jenna looked at the beautiful black haired,green-eyed girl from Salt Lake.

"I'm glad we met, you are like in all my classes."

"I know, it's so nice to have a little friend." Elizabeth told her as she hugged her tight. Sitting down at the table, Jenna told Elizabeth to wait for her and she left. Rock was paying the band, and he turned when she approached.

"Ready to go?" he asked.

She swayed. "I have a favor to ask you, Tiger."

He shook the band manager's hand. "What is it?"

"Elizabeth's friends left her here, can we give her a ride home? It's her birthday."

He nodded. "Let's all go back to the house, I have more champagne there."

"Okay," Jenna said, looking at him with glazed eyes.

The two girls giggled as they stumbled toward the door, one under each of Rock's arms. As the three were walking out, Rock turned to see his brother watching as he left with the hot girls.

"Lucky bastard," a bartender told Rock's brother as they passed by.

"Bastard." The brother muttered one word and walked away.

The giggling girls stumbled into the house hanging on each other and singing a song by Snoop Dogg.

"Snoop, doggie doggie dogg," they sang off key, "Champagne please, lover!"

Rock grinned. "Anything for the two most beautiful women I ever set my eyes upon."

"Charmer!" Elizabeth told Jenna.

"He a tiger," she said she kicked off her shoes and her friend did the same.

Sitting between the two, Rock handed each a full glass of the sugary liquid. While blasting the stereo they drank nearly half the bottle in a few minutes. Jenna and her friend joked and laughed as he watched in amusement at their silly drunkenness. He rubbed both of their necks, and they purred from the strong massage.

"Isn't my man sexy?" Jenna asked her friend.

"I think you are both really sexy," Elizabeth said to Jenna and Rock.

"You know what I think would be really sexy?" He piped in.

"Hmmm?"

"If you two kissed."

Jenna leaned over his lap clumsily as Elizabeth did, at first just playing and flirting with him, but after feeling how soft each others lips felt and tasted, they turned a small peck into full-blown making out.

"Damn, you girls are torturing me," he told them as he sported major hard on.

Suddenly Jenna stopped. "Oh, I want to show you my boots Rock bought me."

They jumped up and ran into the bedroom, leaving Rock, hard and alone and in complete amazement. He followed them into the room. As they looked the boots in the closet, Rock sat on the bed taking off his motorcycle boots and unbuttoning the black rayon shirt. Jenna strutted to the bed in her tall boots, leaned over and kissed Rock's chest.

"Sexy chest!" Jenna said trailing a one finger down his sternum. Elizabeth followed and plopped down on the comforter.

"Do that again," he told them.

Jenna crawled towards her friend as Lizzie, as Jenna called her sometimes, met her half way and the two teased tongues. Rock laid back, took hold of each of their backs, and rubbed up and down on each.

"That is a sexy shirt," Lizzie said as she pulled a string, releasing the barely there top. She passed her tongue over her full lips as the top slid off.

Jenna put her hands over her naked breasts and they all laughed. "Now you have to take off yours, fair is fair."

Whipping it off, along with her bra, Rock pulled the two down to his chest, and kissed each on the lips and they spent the night, experiencing pleasures so dirty, so wild, so unencumbered, so free. They passed the hours entwined like a mating ball of anacondas slithering over each other, around each other, in each other. The following morning, the girls awoke over with a little regret and large hangovers. The pounding from inside their heads was so bad it felt like a jack-hammer going off in their brains.

"Oh my head," Jenna groaned.

Elizabeth crawled from the bed. "I have to go; I have a class at noon."

"Good morning ladies," Rock said. He stood in the doorway holding two bottles of water and aspirin. Rock dispensed the hangover relief to the grateful girls.

"There is a driver outside at your disposal, whenever, no rush."

"Thanks, I think I should go now." Elizabeth sipped water and Rock kissed her cheek.

"Bye," Jenna said from the pillow, unable to lift her head, afraid it would explode.

"Call you later, it was super fun. Thanks." Elizabeth said as she slipped on her dark sunglasses and left.

Falling back asleep after choking down the aspirin, Jenna slept for about an hour and then woke to, find Rock sitting on the patio, drinking black coffee and going over some scripts the studio had sent over for his review. She crawled into his lap and he threw down the script and embraced her tightly.

"How are you feeling?" he asked as he inspected the mark on her neck, not sure if he or Lizzie had caused it.

"Hung over, embarrassed, like a freak and I think I will never drink champagne again, oh did I mention embarrassed?"

He smiled. "Yes, no need to be, I had a good time."

"I bet you did, every man's fantasy." Jenna rolled her eyes.

Rock agreed. "Yes, you are. I wasn't expecting that."

"Me either. You're okay with it?"

"Well, you two nearly gave me a heart attack."

"I try!" She laughed and he did as well. He patted her bum, as she sipped his streaming coffee, burning her lip turning it bright pink.

"Need caffeine of my own." She growled and went off the kitchen.

Oh, please let there be at least one Mountain Dew. Yes, one left. Cracking it open, she drank half the can in one swig. Dragging her body to the couch, Jenna turned on the mammoth television to the entertainment channel. The overly happy announcer spoke to her …

"Stay tuned for sneak peeks of Missy Manga's new movie." Cranking up the volume. Jenna called for Rock rub her back as pictures of some of the stunts flashed across the screen and a close up of Missy's face appeared.

The reporter rambled on, "The outfits, the behind the scenes drama, and Missy's reaction to the untimely death of her assistant."

Jenna switched the channel as Rock entered the room and sat down next to her. He rubbed the back of her neck.

"Oh that feels so good." She nearly purred.

"Yeah? How's this?" he scratched her back from top to bottom, leaving long red marks down her soft smooth back as she laid down over his lap.

"Oh this is better than sex."

He slapped her ass hard.

"Ouch, oh not better than your sweet lovin!"

"That's my girl, I have to get going." He lifted her off his lap and stood to leave.

She pouted. "Where? Stay and keep scratching."

"The club, I have to check on the work they're doing to my office. What's your plan for the day?"

"Nap, eat, sleep, threesome."

He raised his eyebrow. "I'll see you later." He leaned over and kissed her.

Back to bed, she thought and crawled into the big empty bed and fell fast asleep.

"You lazy, dirty girl," Rock joked as he found her still in bed at four o'clock when he returned.

She stretched. "My hangover's gone."

"Let's go down to the beach for a while." Rock suggested, he needed to clear his mind and only two things could do that, sex and surfing.

They spent the rest of the day at Manhattan Beach with Jenna digging her toes into the hot sand and Rock catching a few small waves. Putting her hand over her eyes, she squinted from the late afternoon sun. Checking to see if he caught a wave, Jenna watched him looking so good in his wet suit. Oh, he got one, almost up and no, she laughed as he fell off into the salty ocean water.

As the sun disappeared into the horizon, Jenna wrapped her body in a towel while Rock set logs into a fire pit in the soft sand.

"Man build fire!" he roared and pounded his chest.

"This is so peaceful," she told Rock as he sat behind her and put his long legs around her, hugging her back to his chest.

"I am so glad I moved to California. I love it here, best decision I ever made." He sighed and kissed the back of her neck.

Jenna shivered. "You've never told me where you were from."

"Ohio."

She giggled. "Where the hell is Ohio?"

"Mid-west, south of Detroit."

His hair tickled her cheek. "Oh, never been there." Rock held her tighter.

"And where are you from?" Jenna asked.

"All over."

"There you go, being mysterious again." she half teasing, half-sarcastic.

Just as she was going to push for more information, Rock's cell phone rang out.

"Da," he spoke in his native language and in a few short sentences his demeanor went from cool, calm to rage and anger as he jumped up, walked away towards the parking lot, and then back to her.

"We have to go."

"Okay," she told him in a calm soft-spoken manor. Packing up everything, she put sand on the fire to extinguish it and lugged the storage tub they brought with all the beach goods as Rock went off to take another call. Going back for his surfboard, she carried it to the truck, resting it against the bumper. Waiting in the rear of the truck for him to unlock the door, Jenna listened to Rock's low voice speaking rapidly to the unknown caller. He caught her out of the corner of his eye, pointed the remote, and released the lock for her to load the trunk. Rock was glad she did not question him, he liked that she understood that he just needed her to comply and not probe. Jenna did not want to push him into hitting her again so she tried to stay low-key. He was snarling as they pulled from the parking lot.

She wanted to make him feel better. "I had a good time today, thanks for bring me to the beach."

"Sorry, kiddo, I have to take care of this."

"I understand," she said looking down to the floor mats.

"Tell me," he replied, taking his eyes off the road for a minute to look at her, so cute with her hair up in a high bun and sunglasses perched on top of her head.

"Tell you that I love you?"

"Yes," he said as he took her hand to his lips and kissed the smooth skin on the back of her hand.

"I love you," Jenna said, looking back at him.

"I'm going to drop you off and I'll be back."

"Alright. Rock, you will be careful?"

"Don't worry." He put his hand onto her inner thigh and squeezed.

Speeding up Ventura Blvd. way over the speed limit, Rock answered another call in English this time.

"I told you that I will be there. What!" His tone made Jenna jump in her seat.

Rock stomped heavily on the brakes and swung the truck around. "Change of plans. Hold on," he said as the engine roared and he gunned the accelerator. Jenna held the door frame as he took a sharp left into an industrial park, went through a maze of old run-down buildings and into what looked like a scrap steel grave yard. Feeling sucker punched in the stomach, Jenna's nerves ate away at her belly as Rock barked an order.

"Stay in the truck, understand?"

She nodded, watching his serious expression.

Opening the glove box, he took out a large black nine-millimeter handgun, pulled back the hammer, and loaded the chamber. Opening the door, he climbed out as Jenna looked at him with pleading desperation.

"Stay in the truck," he told her again, put the weapon into his rear waistband, and walked into the warehouse. *What is going on? Oh please, please hurry,* she said in her head. Her nerves were working overtime as every minute seem like a life sentence. For an agonizing twenty minutes, she sat waiting for any sign or sound from the dilapidated old building. Watching the digital clock flip each minute, she tried to keep her leg from shaking. She nearly jumped out of the truck when he emerged.

Jenna searched every inch of his face for any indication of what happened but dared not ask him. He pulled out of the lot quickly, not glancing at her once. Rock was visibly irritated, but his expression turned to stone, as he got further away.

"Are you okay? She asked touching his thigh.

He grabbed her hand tightly. "I'm fine just shut … I'm fine."

She pulled her hand away and shrunk further towards the door, staring out into the passing night.

As the truck slowed for the red light, Rock sighed heavily and spoke. "I didn't mean to snap at you. I wouldn't have brought you here unless it was important."

"You don't have to explain, it's none of my business. In fact, I don't want to know."

He placed his hot hand on the back of her neck and pulled her towards him. Placing his forehead on hers, he breathed a sigh of relief. "You are so perfect, you're the one, don't ever leave me."

Jenna pulled back, looking into his eyes. "I am not perfect and I am not going anywhere, but I don't understand …"

He kissed her roughly as the light turned green, diffusing her line of questioning.

"We need to get home." Rock told her as he pulled away quickly from the light. Jenna gave a long look in his direction, *what is all about?*

Two weeks later, waking earlier than usual, Jenna left Rock sleeping and donned her running shoes. She headed to the gym, burning hard for an hour and a half, taking out as many calories as she could to fit perfect in her coveted new dress. Arriving back, Jenna undressed in the bedroom as Rock woke up to see her naked in front of the closet.

"I got something you can wear," he said in a low growl.

"Oh baby!" Jenna yelled as she jumped into the bed and they made hot fast love and fell back asleep until the doorbell woke both of them.

"That's for you," he said smiling up at her.

"Who is it?"

"A friend of mine; he does hair and make up."

"Oh you are the best, thank you, thank you!" She jumped up and down on the bed, and he grabbed her, sending Jenna to the mattress. Rock kissed her, let her go put on a robe, and she answered the door.

"Geez, I have been like waiting all day. He must have been slipping you his big … Rock, honey daddy's here." The flamboyant hairdresser breezed by her and into the house as Rock walked out of the bedroom wearing only a pair of pajama bottoms, pulling his long hair back into a ponytail.

"Stop teasing me!" the hairdresser went on. "So, what do you want?" Nathan asked Rock, ignoring Jenna.

"You know what I like." Rock replied.

What about what I like? Jenna thought. *Sounds like he's done this before. Maybe I'm not that special after all.* She took a quick shower as Nathan the hairdresser set up his tools and then she was all his for the molding.

"You have great eyes; I will really play them up."

"I'm in your hands," she told Nathan.

After three and a half hours of primping, pulling, fixing and a lot of patience, Jenna emerged of the bedroom looking like a beautiful cross between Marilyn and Madonna a la forty's glamour. Rock dropped his phone to the floor the moment he saw her. He could not believe his eyes, the perfect hair and make up, the short lace covered black dress, and the incredibly high black patent leather stilettos.

He swallowed hard as she approached and gave her million-watt smile from behind red matte lips.

"Perfect. I want to kiss you so bad."

"The lips!" she said as Rock placed one on her neck instead.

Jenna thought, I feel like a million dollars, I hope everything goes okay, this is so exciting. Turning to Nathan she told him, "I've never been to a party like this, I hope I don't trip in these shoes."

"Just keep your ankles straight and you will be fine."

"We have to go, we're late." Rock told her as he put on the black perfectly tailored Armani jacket that matched the trousers he looked so damn fine in.

"You look so dashing, like James Bond," Jenna gushed.

Rock paid Nathan, telling him to let himself out when he was done cleaning up his goods and led her to the shiny black Ferrari that was parked outside in the drive ready to roar.

"Nathan, will you take our picture?"

"Sure kitten." Nathan said as they posed for several photos before he drove slowly down the hill taking care not to mess her hair.

Arriving to the chaos, Jenna felt very overwhelmed at all the hoopla. She wobbled slightly stepping out of the car, and a valet took her hand and winked at her. Walking the red carpet, Jenna had a death grip on her clutch purse and Rock kept his hand on the small of her back as paparazzi snapped a thousand shots. Finally, they escaped and entered the lobby of the ornate oriental-themed theatre.

Rock left her side to speak to some industry people, leaving her standing alone in the sea of actors, directors, media, and other pretentious people.

"Jenna!" A female voice yelled out from behind her. Turning as she heard her name called, Jenna's heart leaped when she saw a familiar face and her friend Elizabeth came rushing over.

"Oh, I am so glad to see you; my date left me to go talk to that lead actress," Lizzie whined.

Jenna nodded. "Me too, Rock is off talking to some guys over there."

Elizabeth winked. "Did you have fun the other night?"

Jenna turned as red as her lipstick. "Yeah, but I'm still embarrassed."

"No worries, we can laugh about it, okay?"

"Sure, how come you're here?" Jenna asked Elizabeth.

"I work for the company across the street, the real estate company that is going to put a huge mall next to this theatre. The re-birth of Hollywood, it's going to really cool."

"Tell me about it later; let's go get a drink, but no champagne! And then I want to introduce you to my friend Scotty." Jenna nodded towards Scotty, who was talking to Jared.

"Is he the Italian stud over there?" Elizabeth's eyes widened.

"Yup."

Her friend made a purring noise. "I want him! He is so hot."

"Come on ..."

Elizabeth and Scotty's chemistry was visibly charged; they hit it off instantly and Jenna left the two to find her own man.

Rock, being so tall, could see over the crowd and watched her looking around for him. He watched as men stopped in their tracks as she sauntered by not once looking at any of them, only having eyes for him. Good, he thought, that's my girl. He continued to monitor her as she ran into Tracy and had a long conversation with her. He read her lips as Jenna told her friend. No, I have to find Rock. What do you mean he left? He told you to tell me and then take me home? He watched intently as Tracy replied, saying something about an emergency, to stay with her and he will be right back.

Rock's brow furrowed. Why would she tell Jenna I left?

In a single moment, his survival instincts kicked in. He knew. Knew that she was the one who tried to kill Jenna on set. Pushing aside a waiter, Rock rushed across the room, but they girls were gone by the time he made his way through the crowd.

Stepping into the tunnel under the theatre, the hair on Jenna's arms rose as Tracy led her further away from the noise of the party.

"I don't think we should be down here," Jenna said, looking around.

"No, it's okay, we'll just take the elevator up and look around real quick, we'll be back in ten minutes, no one will even know were gone," Tracy assured her.

"We have a problem." Rock pulled Scotty aside from Lizzie. Whispering in his ear, Rock filled told him quickly as he could. Scotty apologized to Lizzie and gave her his phone to hold onto. The two men moved quickly through the parking lot to Scotty's car, loaded up on weapons and went to the construction project entrance where he last saw Jenna and Tracy walking and talking.

Jenna's stilettos wobbled across the unfinished floor in the shell of the future hotel. Piles stacks of lumber and building materials lined the halls and empty shells of rooms where Tracy led her.

"I don't think we should be up here," Jenna repeated.

Tracy just grinned. "It's just a little farther, come on, I want to show you the view from the prototype room."

Jenna stopped. "I need to get back and find Rock. I can see it another time."

As she said the words, she felt cold, hard steel on her back.

"You're not going anywhere, bitch."

Turning around slowly, Jenna put her hands up and stared in sheer disbelief at the girl who she thought was her friend pointing a gun at her. "Tracy, what are you doing?"

"Well dumb bunny, I am trying to kill you. Since my other attempts seemed to fail, I thought I would take a more direct approach."

Jenna blinked. "But ... Why? I thought we were friends?"

Tracy waved the gun. "Blood is thicker than water. If you haven't figured it out yet, Missy is my younger sister, and I take offense when someone gets in the way of what she wants."

Jenna swallowed, looking at the barrel. "And she wants Rock?"

"I'd do anything to make her happy. And now what would make her happy is to see you dead," Tracy said, smiling.

"That's right; I always get what I want. And I have waited along time to run into you again."

A voice coming out of the shadows spoke. Missy stepped into light so Jenna could see her face snickering at her.

"Oh, yeah, sorry about the car, the career, the lawsuit, finding me in Rock's bed." The sisters laughed wickedly as Jenna wrapped her arms around her shivering body. Now she saw the family resemblance in their demonic faces.

Missy wetted her lips. "Oh don't worry; I'm going to console Rock when he finds out you killed yourself. I am going to console him all night long, every night. He'll be screaming my name when he comes."

Acidy liquid perched into her throat, but she swallowed in the best she could, trying to remain calm, so the girls would not sense her fear. "No, he will never be with you. Why him, you could have any man?"

"I like a challenge. Plus, it will be good publicity for the movie and my career," the pop tart told Jenna as she walked around her, circling like a wolf stalking it prey.

"You're sick, both of you," Jenna said to the sisters.

They cackled like witches as Jenna looked around for an escape route. She tried to slip out of the shoes, but Missy saw her movement.

"What are you doing?" Tracy said nervously.

"These shoes are killing me," Jenna apologized, hoping to buy time.

"Fitting words for a girl about to meet her fate," Missy said.

"I have a party to get back to. Take care of this, so I can go find my man." Missy walked to Jenna and stopped in front of her. "I can't wait to do him; I heard he's a real good in bed."

Jenna had enough; if she was going to die, it would not be without a struggle.

Snatching the actress by the throat, she reached around and took hold of her from the back. Missy screamed as Tracy fired the weapon impulsively, barely missing Missy and sending a bullet into the wall.

"You almost shot me, you dumb ass!" The actress screamed at her sister as Jenna released her and pushed her towards Tracy. Jenna ran as fast as she could through the labyrinth of beams and studs. Still in the heels, her feet screamed and stopping to take them off, she hurried as she held them tight and hid behind a wall listening for footsteps.

Hearing the gun shot, Rock and Scotty cocked their weapons and headed up into the direction of the blast. As they ascended the steps, Missy ran down, stopping as she saw the armed men heading up the stairs and blocking her escape route. She scrambled away in the opposite direction. At the top of the steps, the men nodded at each other and parted ways to look for the girls.

"Come out here, you whore!" Tracy taunted Jenna. "I am going to kill you once I find you, so why delay the inevitable?"

Jenna stood frozen in the hiding spot she had found. Looking through the project, she could see a shadowy form moving towards her. *I could run, but which direction*? Wait a minute, that figure is taller than Missy and Tracy, she thought as she continued to watch the movement of the shadow. Into view came her rescuer, Rock, who stepped out of the darkness, weapon drawn, looking very cautiously around each corner. I have to get his attention somehow without being shot. Taking the shiny shoe, she tried to shine the light in his direction. He saw, closed one eye, and pointed the weapon at the tiny hand that was holding the shoe. *Well, he has not shot, I am just going to stick my head out a little,* she thought. Rock lowered his nine-millimeter weapon and she mouthed a help to him. He motioned to her to stay down as he checked the room before moving toward her.

Scotty crept around, not seeing any sign of anyone. His special forces training had fine-tuned his hearing to be able to tell a person's, height, and weight just by listening. He felt he was closing on someone but not female. With a slight whistle, he commanded Rock's attention and the two men acknowledged each other with nods and hand signals.

Quietly slipping behind Jenna, Tracy grabbed her by the hair and screamed. "Got you! Time to die bitch; I'm going to kill you just like Missy's incompetent assistant!"

Jenna struggled with Tracy, grabbing her wrist that was holding the weapon and twisted it around as they both vied for control of the twenty-two caliber gun.

"You stupid whore!" Tracy yelled as the two men positioned, waiting for a clear shot even thought they hated to fire at the young girl. Scotty signaled to Rock to cover him, but it was too late, the pistol went off with a loud pop.

"Oh shit! You shot me!" Missy cried as she collapsed on the floor, clutching her chest. Tracy stood staring at her sister in shock. She loosened the grip on the pistol and Jenna knocked it to the ground.

Scotty knelt down and felt Missy's neck for a pulse. "She's dead." He looked up at Tracy who was shaking her head in denial. Suddenly, Tracy lunged for the gun.

They all screamed at once. "NO!"

Scotty and Rock raised their weapons but it was too late, Tracy put the gun to her temple and fired.

Through the shock and dust came sounds of sirens and footsteps. Rock grabbed Jenna and pulled her away from where she stood staring at the two lifeless bodies. There were voices calling to them, and the three ran in the opposite direction.

"My shoes!" Jenna yelled.

"Fuck the shoes," Rock answered, dragging her across the floor.

"No, they will know there was someone else was here." She ran back towards the crime scene.

"Shit, she's right." Scotty said to Rock, "It won't look like a simple murder-suicide."

Jenna made it to the shoes but slipped in the blood and tripped over a body.

"Freeze, let me see your hands!" The officer called out as he spotted Jenna lying next to the dead girls bodies.

"I tried to stop her," was all Jenna could say.

From a distance, the two men listened as the officer asked who else was here, and Jenna told the officer no one else.

"I tried to reason with her, but she went crazy and killed Missy then killed herself." Jenna cried.

"Calm down, you're going to be alright." The officer took pity on Jenna who was crying and shaking in warm pools of blood.

"Let's go." Rock said to Scotty as more police arrived and started to spread out.

"We can't leave her," Scotty protested.

"There's nothing we can do to help." Rock took a back way out. He knew Scotty was right not to leave but did not want to risk attention. The less people included the quicker this would blow over. Scotty followed Rock through the passage to the party. They continued as if nothing happened and acted surprised about all the commotion going on. Rock and Scotty answered a few questions like the rest of the party goers and were released quickly unlike Jenna who Rock claimed was merely an acquaintance and had worked with on the movie.

After an hour at the scene, the officers took Jenna downtown for more questioning and a statement. It just happened that the two detectives who had questioned her before caught this case.

"Well, well, look who we have here." Rafferty quipped as he entered the interrogation room. Jenna shivered in the cold puke-green colored room, as one of the two detectives pulled out a chair turned it backwards, sat next to her and looked at her still covered in the dead girls' blood. He sized her up for a moment, stood, and put his sport coat over her bare shoulders. Good cop, bad cop she thought. Jenna might be naïve but she knew this routine from the movies she watched.

"So, why don't you tell us what really happened?" Rafferty, the good cop asked her.

"I told you. How many times do I have to repeat myself?" Jenna countered.

"As many times as I ask you!" Detective Best, her choice for bad cop said, slamming his fist on the table, making Jenna jump in her chair.

"Where's your boyfriend? Why isn't he here to get you? Did he abandon you?" Best grilled her.

Jenna glared at him. "He had nothing to do with this. He was at the party—probably wondering what happened to me!"

"You think he really cares about you? What exactly do know about him anyways?" Bad cop prodded.

"Enough Best, go get her a soda or something and cool your jets."

Bad cop left the room, and good cop tried to sway her with his sympathy.

"Look, I know it was scary and I am here to help you, just tell me what really happened and you can go home," Rafferty said in a soft, kind, very rehearsed tone.

"I told you the truth, please can I go now?" she begged the detective as his partner returned.

"Can I use the phone?" Jenna asked Rafferty who returned and sat on the edge of the table.

"Constantine got a hot shot lawyer for you?" Detective Best taunted her.

"No, I want to call Rock."

"She wants to call Rock. Her boyfriend. How sweet," Best said sarcastically. Taking her out to his desk, he let Jenna make one call. Jenna's eyes filled to the brim as the voice mail told her that he was not accepting any calls at this time.

Hours of intense interrogation led Best and Rafferty to the conclusion that they were not getting anywhere with her story; she was telling the truth. Her fingerprints were not on the gun, so they released her into the cold morning light.

Jenna shivered. Dressed only in the mini dress and spiked heels, she waited for someone to come get her but no one did. Never feeling so alone or so tired, she walked slowly to the curb. No money, no purse, no cell phone and too much pride to go back in to ask to use the phone, Jenna waited on the street corner hoping Rock would fetch her, but he never did. Finally, a lonely taxi pulled up slowly as she walked down the street.

"Lady, need Taxi?" The foreign driver asked her as he raised his eyebrows, raising his turban.

"Yes, Hollywood Hills, please."

On the ride home, the taxi driver tried to make conversation, but all Jenna could think of how abandoned she felt by Rock and Scotty. It's my own fault, I should have listened to him. Telling him to wait she went in to retrieve cab fare and took it back out to the waiting driver.

Closing the door to the house, Jenna looked at the clock. Five-fifty nine in the morning. The cold darkness filled the room, leaving Jenna feeling desolate and alone. As she sat down wearily on the sofa, she ran her hands over her face and blew out a long breath. She sat staring into the nothingness of the room, not thinking any certain thought. Standing up to go into the bedroom, she nearly jumped out of her skin as a hand touched her shoulder. Too tired to fight, Jenna turned around to face him. He simply stared down at her, both stood silent. Since Rock said nothing Jenna turned and walked past him into the bedroom, undressed and went into the shower, washing off the make up and washing the fancy hair do out and the blood that stained her skin. The cool water ran over her body, numbing her physically and matching the deadness of her emotions. Trying to process the anger, confusion, sadness of it all, Jenna turned off the water, wrapped a towel around her, and went into the bedroom to find Rock sitting on the edge of the bed. Jenna thought—it's because of me that Missy wanted Rock. I'm the reason Tracy tried to kill him and me. If it wasn't for me, he'd be happy, his life would be less complicated, she contemplated for a moment and decided, I can not make his life miserable, I have caused too much trouble.

"I have probably ruined your career and life. I think it's best if I leave."

Rock sat silent, after a minute, stood, and crossed his arms. "If that's what you want, so be it." The hurtful words stung hard but he did not mean it, he wanted her to stay, but foolish pride got in the way and he did not retract his words.

Jenna lowered her head and turned to the closet, dressed, knelt down, and started to pack some clothes into a duffle bag. When she finished, he looked at her realizing she was really going to leave. Rock's face snarled with ire and he put his fist in the dresser mirror, shattering it to a thousand pieces sending her nervous into instant overdrive.

Pain! Jenna gasped and grabbed her sides. Something was wrong, in her womb. The pain seared her brain and she felt blackness pulling at her. Jenna called for Rock as she fell to the floor.

He heard her low cry, "Rock … ughh."

At first, Rock was not going to run back to her, but changed his mind when he heard the need in her voice. He could hear the sound of the thud her body made as it hit the ground. Rushing into the room, he saw her crumpled body on the floor next to the bed. Realizing she something more serious than her fainting was going on, he turned her over and slapped her pale ash colored face repeatedly, trying to awake her.

"Kiddo, wake up." Rock called out to her. His gut felt like he took a hard blow to it when he saw blood pouring out quickly from between her legs. Rock gasped at the site, and ran his hand through his hair trying to think what to do. Rushing in to the bathroom, Rock opened the cabinet, grabbed a large towel, and rushed back to her. Shoving the towel in between her legs, he scooped her up into his arms and ran her out to the truck, placing her gently in the front seat. He did think the ambulance could get to them faster than if he drove her to the hospital himself.

"Rock, what's happening?" She asked, but slumped against the door before he could tell her.

"Unfortunately the news is not good," The doctor told Rock as he came out of the examination room. "She's had a miscarriage. It was two months into the pregnancy. The stress was too much. There was nothing we could have done, I'm sorry."

Rock ran his hands down his face and listened intently to the doctor. "I think it would be in her best interest to keep her for a few days; she's extremely mentally fragile, and in need of rest."

Rock thanked the doctor and went behind the curtain to find Jenna lying on her side staring blankly at the wall.

"Are you alright?" Rock asked, not knowing what to say. Closing her eyes, her chin quivered before she broke into full-blown sobs. Rock watched, unsure how to comfort her. Rock reached for Jenna but she pushed his hand away. Reaching again, he put a firmer grip on her shoulder, pulling her to him. Throwing her arms around him, she wept uncontrollably as he held her tight and tried to soothe her.

"Everything happens for a reason, it just wasn't meant to be," he spoke softly to her. "Why didn't you tell me?"

"I didn't know, I would have told you, I would not have kept from you, I swear. Oh Rock I am so sorry, sorry for everything. I tried to be strong; I just don't know if I can go on anymore." She sobbed hard into his chest.

"You've been through more tonight than most in a lifetime."

"Please take me home, I want to go home, now," Jenna begged.

He sighed and kissed the top of her head. "You can't go home tonight; you need to rest for awhile, on a nice quiet floor."

"No, no don't do this, please, I am not crazy, Rock you can't let them keep me." She clutched his shirt.

"It's just for few days, to rest." He brushed at her hair.

"No, Rock, my baby, please, no … I am not staying here, those girls are dead, my baby's dead, I want to be dead with my baby!"

Jenna tried to climb out of the bed, attempted to pull the IV from her arm, and brought the nurse and orderly running to check on the ruckus. She flung her arms out and turned over the chair next to the bed.

"Jenna, calm down!" Rock shouted, watching the mental unraveling of his lover before his eyes. As the orderly held her down, the nurse pulled out a large syringe and stuck Jenna's arm, sedating her.

"My baby, I want my baby …" she whimpered as she drifted off into a deep sedative-induced slumber. Rock stood in shock. The staff strapped her to the bed with large leather and metal restraints about the wrists and feet.

"I'm sorry, Jenna," Rock said to her unconscious body and walked out just like her father had done years before.

In the six months that passed, the physical wounds healed, but emotional ones still held lightly covered scabs. Cleared of any wrongdoing in the murder-suicide, she survived the hounding of the press, all the tabloids stories, and the constant guilt that loomed over her. While Jenna worked full time for her friend Lizzie she continued with a full schedule at University of Southern California, throwing herself into as many classes as possible. She even attended weeknight and all day Saturday class. Purposely leaving little time for herself, let alone Rock, Jenna managed to take care of the house all the while balancing school and work. They lived more like roommates than lovers with Rock on location and rarely home. She missed that he stopped trying to making love, although Jenna reminded herself that she always shot down his advances. Sex was too scary for her now; she was afraid of getting pregnant and going through the same horrible trauma again. So she never gave him any indication that she was interested and he knew she would probably reject him again if he asked, so why bother?

Therapy helped but didn't heal. She worked through the confusion and rejection but could not rid herself of the abandonment she felt from her father and especially from Rock.

Time passed as Rock was gone for over three weeks while in Canada shooting a sequel to one of his previous movies, which he now had the lead part. The quiet house made her long for him. At night, she could almost hear his breathing next to her in bed, smell the musky fragrance of his cologne, and hear him calling her name. She longed again to be that young girl in love. Wanting him to be waiting for her when she came home from class waiting with flowers, bubble baths and surprises.

One day spent like the others, studying after work, watching TV and cleaning up around the house Jenna finally felt it was time to do something nice for herself. Taking a long bath, shaving her legs and pampering herself a little, she felt her spirits lift slightly, enough to make her want to slip on a silky nightie and feel a little sexy. Jenna walked out of the bathroom to find Rock. Sitting on the edge of the bed looking weary, she froze as if she had seen a ghost.

They stared at each other like deer in headlights; Jenna shocked to see him home; Rock amazed to find her in the sexy nightie.

"I didn't hear you come in. When did you get back?" Jenna asked.

"Just now," he told her, still staring at the bare legs under the short purple gown.

As if it were normal, she leaned over and kissed him on the lips in a nice welcome home way. Shocked at her behavior, he reciprocated with one of his own.

Blushing slightly, Jenna tucked the hair behind her ear, as he stood to take off his coat. Jenna helped him pull it off and took the coat to the closet for him. She hung it up, and turned back to see him taking off his shirt, wincing painfully.

"Rough shoot?" she asked.

"Yeah, the flight was long and I couldn't sleep on the plane." He sat nervously on the edge of the bed.

When he bent over to untie his boots, Jenna stopped him. "Let me do that." She knelt in front of him, unlaced the combat boots, removed his socks, stood, and put them away. She barely even made him coffee anymore, he thought, but he was thankful and surprised at how attentive she was being.

"I'm going to shower," he said getting up, walking past her.

"Are you hungry? I could make something for you."

Rock stopped in his tracks and looked at her, "No, too tired to eat, but thank you."

He turned away to shower. Jenna sat on the edge of the bed lifted his shirt to her nose and drank in the scent of him. The mix of sweat and cologne stirred something inside her that she had not felt in months. Pulsations zapped between her legs as she laid back on the bed, remembering nights of hot sweaty sex and how he made her come hard every time. Getting up to put the shirt into the hamper, she ran smack into his naked chest.

"Oh," she panted, "Sorry". He lifted her chin to look into her eyes, the beautiful greenish-brown orbs he fell so hard for in the beginning. As she put her hand on his soaking wet chest, the sexual feelings deep inside her womb stirred.

Taking her arms, he rubbed his hands from her elbows up to her shoulders, feeling every inch of her skin. God she felt amazing, he thought. Rock slipped his finger under the spaghetti strap of the satin nightie, sending it down to rest on her bicep. He continued to trace his finger along her collarbone, down her sternum and between her breasts, which were now at full attention. As the other strap fell from her shoulder, she closed her eyes as he leaned down, planting a gentle kiss on each shoulder. With palms flat, she rubbed her hands over his arms, down his chest, over his six-pack abs and down to the spot just before the path of dark hair started. In a slow, gentle manor, he lifted her up into his arms and kissed her softly as he placed her down onto the bed. Thundering shocks of electricity bolted between them as he lifted off the nightgown and she removed his towel. The chemistry was uncontrollable and it consumed them like when they first met.

"I feel like this is the first time," she told him, as he lay over her naked body.

Rock touched her cheek. "I know, are you nervous?"

"Yes, are you?"

"Yes. Oh god, Jenna, I want you, I need you." His head pounded with emotions and lust. All he wanted to do was show her how much he loved her. He longed to be inside her and he could not wait another second.

"I want to make love to you now," he said in a hard, breathy voice.

Jenna felt between his legs and guided him to her hot flesh folds. Her insides quivered as he placed the tip to her opening, gently entering her. Squeaking as he tried, she begged him to fill her but it was tight and he was so engorged.

"I'm trying, does it hurt?" He asked her as she seized his ass and roughly thrust him into her. They both gasped in pleasuring pain. Jenna reached out clutching the bedspread as he plunged into her over and over. Going deeper with every move, Rock nearly lost consciousness as the feeling him inside her, was so overwhelming and engulfing.

"Oh, you feel good, Jenna, so fucking good." He said as he closed his eyes and tilted back his head holding himself as far in her as he could. He kept the position for a few seconds to control the desire to let the river flow. After a few minutes, he continued his sliding in and out, as Jenna got a hold of one of his nipples and sucked on it. He started to come as the sensation of her tongue flicked over his nipple. Pulling out, he filled her belly button so much it over flowed on her abdomen and on the bed. Taking his boxers, he wiped her clean, and laid over her.

"What do you want me to do, to for you?" he asked wanting her to be satisfied.

"I just want you to tell me," she whispered.

"I love you." he finally told her and he could not hold back tears when he saw hers.

"I thought you didn't love me," Jenna told him as she wiped her cheeks. Jenna sat up and he followed.

"I really expected to come home to an empty house. You surprised me when you walked out of the bathroom."

"I was shocked to see you too. Oh tiger, you are my everything, my world, my love. You are my Rock."

He moved from the bed to the closet, fished around in his coat pocket, and brought something back to the bed. Jenna covered up with the top sheet as he came back and pulled her up out of the bed. Jenna stood, the sheet draping over her body as he knelt on one knee.

"I was going to give you this the night of the premier. Jenna, I love you, have since the first moment I saw you on set. You have opened my heart, you own it. I would be honored if you would have me for all eternity. Will you marry me?"

Shaking hands covered her mouth as her eyes went from his face to the box and back to his face. "Yes, I want to, I will marry you!"

The square cut three-carat stone, sparkled brightly, lighting up the room as he took it out and slid it over her knuckle. Jenna ravished his mouth as tears of joy flood both of their eyes.

They wed in a simple ceremony attended only by her friend Elizabeth and Scotty. Rock and Jenna stood on the black sands of Oahu, giving each other vows of love, trust and forever as the sun set on the most perfect day they had ever spent together. They lived in happiness for the first year, acting like newly weds every chance they could, making love wherever, whenever they could.

"When are you going to be home?" Rock asked Jenna one afternoon.

"Soon, why? You want me to cook?"

"No, I have to run down to Scotty's house to go over a new movie proposal. He has a huge action film he wants me to do. I thought we could make a weekend of it, go to that Mexican restaurant you like."

"Mario's!" I'm pulling in the drive now." She snapped closed the phone and whipped into the driveway, pulling her shopping bags from the trunk. She lugged them into the house and went directly to the bedroom.

"Tiger? I'm home. Are you naked?"

"No, what did you buy me?"

"Three hundred-count sheets, a pink thong and Japanese Cherry blossom candles."

"I can't wait to test out those sheets," he said, coming up behind Jenna and mauling her playfully.

"Stop, my husband will be home any minute."

"What, you're married? I feel so used!" They laughed at the little role playing they loved to do.

"Get packed. We'll stay till Sunday."

"Really? I just love it Orange County when are we going to move there?"

"Tell you what, as soon as I finish this movie we'll buy our perfect house, right across from the beach."

"Deal."

After packing their things, Jenna drove them in her Volkswagen. Friday traffic was a bear, as everyone was fleeing the city all at once. Rock put his seat all the way back and fell asleep for half the ride, as Jenna tooled her way down Interstate Five. Jenna sang along with Madonna's latest album, hitting one very high note off key and waking Rock from his nap.

"Did I hear cats fighting?" he asked.

"Funny, you should have been a comedian," she said dryly.

"Do you realize we haven't had sex in three days?" He said, taking her fingers and kissing each individually.

Jenna shrugged. "We haven't?"

"I'm having withdrawals." He watched the way she was holding the stick shift wishing she had a hold of his stick in the same fashion.

"I'll give you a withdrawal alright." Jenna slid one hand down into this track suit bottoms and kept the other on the wheel. Rock put his arms behind his head as he lay back on the seat and let her take hold of his manhood. Her warm little hands touched the soft smooth skin of his stiffening rod. Running her fingertips across over his tip, she stroking the end, gripping it tight making him squirm in the passenger seat. Licking his lips, he opened his mouth, closed his eyes as her touch sent the millions of nerve endings in to over drive. Now fully hard and begging for her lips, Rock took it out as Jenna looked around to make sure no other cars could see. Working the shaft with one hand, she listened to her favorite thing to hear, him groaning in pleasure. Working it faster with each stroke, he seeped out a little onto her finger and Rock watched as she took it to her mouth and tasted making him mad with lust. Taking her hand off him to downshift as she exited the freeway onto Springdale Avenue, Rock continued the job himself reaching over and feeling between her legs over her shorts.

"I have to taste you." She said as she pulled away from the exit ramp and quickly onto the first side street she found. Whipping the Jetta over to the curb in front of one unsuspecting homeowner, pulling up the emergency brake, unbuckled her seat belt practically diving out of her seat took take him into her mouth.

Rock looked around be fore closing his eyes and letting her devour him with amazing voracity. Bobbing her mouth over his sizeable shaft, the heated saliva helped him slid so far in her touched the back of her throat, which made him cum so hard it felt like his balls exploded. He growled as she squeezed his sac right as he lost his load. He moaned as his wife sucked every drop from him until it hurt.

"Stop." He said and she lifted her head and swallowed, threw the car into first gear, took off the brake and zoomed out of the neighborhood and back down Springdale to the PCH.

"Did any one see us?"
"Do you really care?"
"No at all."
"My wife, you never cease to amaze me."
"My husband, sexist man alive."

Slowing the car to a roll, Jenna drove past a little fruit stand she always stopped at when they were in Orange County and pulled into get a few things.

"I'll only be a minute."

"Hey, get bananas."

Sauntering past the hood, Jenna walked away and into the stand. From behind the windshield, Rock watched his wife. How did I ever get so lucky? Maybe I should not do this movie, maybe I should stay here, find some work. Three months is a long time to be away. Maybe I can fly Jenna out as soon as classes are done.

"What's got you so far away?" she asked, opening the back door to put her purchase on the seat.

"I am not sure I want to leave you for three months."

She climbed into the driver's seat. "Soon as finals are over I'll come and join you. It's only a month or so into the shoot."

"And hopefully you'll have a son with you," he said, putting his hand on her belly.

"What if I can't ... I lost one." She looked at the steering wheel.

"Don't say that, one way or another, someday you are going to have my child."

"I can't wait." She leaned over and tried to kiss him.

He stopped her. "I don't know where that mouth has been."

"If you ever want it to go there again you better give up the lips."

He kissed her quickly as she started the car. They continued towards Scotty's beachfront home.

The men spent the weekend discussing the movie as Jenna and Elizabeth lounged on the beach, and spent hours shopping. They all had a lovely good-bye Sunday night before heading up to their house in Los Angeles. Jenna was so happy that Scotty and Elizabeth were living together and very happy. She would have Elizabeth to lean when Rock left for this next project with Scotty and vice versa.

It was misery when Rock and Jenna had to part. They tried so hard to start a family before Rock headed to Europe but as he left, she was still not pregnant. Saying goodbye this time was the most difficult parting they had ever done. Neither Jenna nor Rock knew why, and could not explain it. Lying in bed in the early morning hours, Rock rubbed her back as he held her close, both shedding silent tears onto each other's skin.

"Don't think of it as good bye, just a see ya later," he told her, kissing his wife's head.

Jenna sighed. "Promise you will call when you can?"

"Of course, I will be thinking of you every moment."

Life went on as normally for the both of them, Jenna attending classes and working; Rock coordinating the fight scenes and training his supporting actors to fight him, until the fated day, a month into the shoot.

Jenna awoke alone feeling slightly weary. Scotty and Rock were off in an Eastern European remote location shoot; Jenna was finishing her final class and was planning to visit in two weeks. Only one week until graduation with her bachelors in business, with a minor in finance, she thought, I have worked damn hard for this.

Days turned into weeks since she had heard from her husband, and graduation had come and gone. The remoteness of the location and the heavy shooting schedule prevented many of the phone calls but she knew he would call as soon as he could. Jenna could not book her flight until she talked to her husband. It left Jenna feeling uneasy and anxious. Her friend Elizabeth brought over a grand Marnier cake and the two caught up, dished, and shared how much they missed their men. The phone rand and Jenna ran to get it.

"Hello, Rock?"

She was surprised to hear Scotty's voice. "Jenna, honey its Scotty."

"Hey Scotty, Elizabeth's here and we were just saying how much we missed you guys."

He ignored her happy chatter. "Listen to me, this is important, have you seen or heard from Rock?"

Her skin went cold. "No not in like two weeks. Why, Scotty? You're scaring me."

His voice faltered. "I don't know how to tell you this ..."

"Tell me what?" She nearly shouted the words.

"It's Rock ... he's gone."

Jenna choked. "Gone? What do you mean gone, do not say that, it's not funny."

Scotty sounded weary. "He's been missing for days; no one has seen or heard from him for over a week. Jenna, we called the police, did a missing person's report, the whole thing, but he has not shown up for work. He never does that."

"No, he's probably coming here. You're wrong," Jenna said in denial.

"Jen, his wallet, and passport were still in his room. Honey, I am so sorry."

The last thing Jenna remembered was dropping the phone and going numb.

Days passed slowly, tortured nights dragged on, as Jenna waited for any word of his whereabouts, but no word ever came from her husband. Anguish and worry ate away any appetite she had. Jenna sat on the floor of the bedroom holding on one of his shirts drinking in the last of the lingering scent of him. Her head was clouded, her body felt hollow, her heartbroken as if it was stabbed repeatedly. It had happened once again, as soon as she gave over her complete heart it was ripped out of her chest as she felt abandoned just as if had been her father leaving her instead of Rock. Nothing could ever take this feeling away; it grew stronger every moment she had to endure without her husband. Jenna desperately cried, please don't leave me alone. I don't want to be alone. But it was useless Rock like her father was not coming back.

"Scotty, I'm worried, Jenna hasn't returned my call in two days." Elizabeth told Scotty in a phone conversation, as he sat in the airport in Phoenix waiting on an hour layover for his flight back to LAX. This trip home had been arduous flying from Europe.

"That's not like her to not call you back." Scotty said checking his watch.

"I can't leave work right now; can you stop there on your way to my house?"

"Sure, I bet she's just busy." He hoped it was true.

When Scotty returned to Los Angeles, he went was directly to Rock's house to see Jenna. Seeing her car in the drive, he went to check on his friend.

"Jen? Honey you here?"

Oddly, he found the door unlocked. Walking in, Scotty looked around for any sign of his friend. Something about the eerie quiet made the hairs on the back of his neck stand on end. Searching the kitchen and living room, he found no sign of her. Scotty entered the bedroom last and was horrified at what he saw in front of him. Lying on the floor was an empty pill bottle, and Jenna limp body.

"Jesus, Jenna what the hell did you do?" he screamed at her. Checking for a pulse, he felt a slight beat but she at least had one, he thought as he pick up the bottle, read the label and threw it down again. He tapped her face to wake her. Lifting her up off the floor, Scotty dragged her body into the bathroom, turned on the ice-cold water, threw her into the tub, and stuck his finger down her throat. Gagging violently, Jenna purged her stomach contents, not stopping until every bit expelled out. Freezing cold water shocked her back to reality and she started to cry.

"I can't go on without him. Let me go … I can't!" she shouted hysterically, sobbing, weeping. Scotty pulled her out of the tub and held her as she shivered violently. Clutching each other, tears flowed from out of both of their eyes. Scotty stroked her cheek and she buried her face in his chest.

"You'll come with me and I'll get you some help. Okay? Jenna, you need help."

She shook her head. "I need my husband, where is he? Tell me where he is."

"I don't know, he's my best friend, and he's gone." Scotty replied tears streaming down his tanned face.

"Take me out of here … I can not be in this house another minute," Jen pleaded with him, her voice strained.

"Alright, come on." He helped her to her feet and took her to the bedroom.

Pulling the comforter off the bed, he wrapped it around her gaunt body and led her out to the taxi he had asked to wait for him. His sadness turned to anger as he jumped in next to her, taking a quick glace at her profile. However, seeing the defeated soul of her, he felt pity and reached over her. Placing his hand over hers, he squeezed but Jenna did not respond, just sat staring straight ahead. Damn stupid what she did, he thought, but did not convey his feelings with her fragile state.

Scotty called Elizabeth to tell her they were driving straight to the little bungalow she had purchased in Silver Lake. Meeting them at the door, Elizabeth took one look at Jenna and did not to ask any questions. Enclosing her into her arms, Lizzie led Jenna directly into the spare bedroom and tucked her into her soft, comfortable bed. Stroking her hair, Elizabeth told Jenna to sleep and promised that they would talk in to the morning. Jenna gave a simple defeated nod and closed her eyes.

Elizabeth closed the door and turned to Scotty. "What happened?"

He sighed slowly. "She downed a bunch of pills. Jenna said that could not live with out Rock."

"Oh, no! She's been so strong, until today, I wonder what happened to push her over the edge ... What's today's date?"

"June thirteenth, why?" Scotty asked.

"Their one year anniversary," Elizabeth said sadly.

"Awe, damn it," he said, looking at the door to the spare bedroom.

His girlfriend wiped at a tear. "I have an acquaintance that is a shrink, I will call her in the morning, make her an appointment."

"I've never seen her far gone, she's been through so much and always had hope and a good attitude and now ..."

"She lost the love of her life, her husband. I feel so bad for my little friend; we're all she has now." Elizabeth sighed. "And how are you coping? You've lost your best friend."

Elizabeth stretched out her arms around his neck and he pulled her close to him.

"I'll be fine, I'm more worried about Jenna, Oh baby, I missed you," he said nuzzling into her his voice now strained with sad weariness.

"I missed you too, let's go to bed, it's been a long day. But Scotty what happened, where's Rock?"

"I think his past caught up with him, look there is a side to him that ... well, only a select few know about. I can't go into detail, but let's just say." Scotty paused hard. "We may never know what happened."

"You think he's dead?"

"I have no idea. I have to assume the worst." Scotty said tore up. Elizabeth lead him to bed and consoled him.

As a new day dawned, Jenna awoke feeling as if she had slept a hundred years. Walking out of the spare bedroom, Jenna found her two friends sitting closely on the couch and they stood up as she approached.

"I just want to apologize for putting you both through ..." she swallowed hard holding back the tears. "I did a stupid, selfish thing and I am sorry."

As she stopped speaking, Scotty began to speak and she held up her hand to stop him.

"I've decided that I need professional help, I'm going to check myself in," Jenna said.

"You made the right decision, and we will be here for you," Scotty told her and hugged her tightly.

"Thank you, I love you both. I am so blessed to have friends like you." She let out a small sob, went to clean herself and Elizabeth loaned her clothes that hung on her skinny frame.

An hour later she checked into the hospital.

Four going on five years passed since the disappearance of her husband. Jenna created a new life for herself, happy on her own, contently working for the real estate developer building the new home of the Oscars. Jenna obtained her Masters degree in business and never looked back to the best and worst time of her life. Instead, she tucked the memories away in her mind as she always did in order to cope.

"Come on we have to be at the Oscar party by seven if we want to get a seat by Clooney." Her friend Elizabeth yelled to her as they rushed out the door.

"I know, but it took me forever to get in this Cavelli dress."

"You look great in Emerald green. Maybe you will meet your future husband at the party tonight." Elizabeth joked.

"Maybe, I think it's time now to get back out there and see what it waiting for me."

"Come on stunt girl, were going to be late." Elizabeth said. She checked out the window as Scotty pulled up in his Land Rover.

"This party is great!" Elizabeth squeaked as they climbed into the car.

"That guy keeps starring at me." Jenna said as they stood holding drinks.

"Which one?" Elizabeth asked swirling around.

"Tan, slicked-back hair, super model type." Jenna said, flashing her eyes in dashing man's direction.

"You do know who that is, don't you?" Scotty asked.

"No, who is he?" Jenna inquired as she studied the gorgeous man.

"Sheridan Stone, he is one of the richest record producers in Hollywood and he's coming this way." Elizabeth turned Jenna around as he approached, her eyes captured by the man's haunting eyes.

He stared at her in the same way. "I am mesmerized. Sheridan Stone, pleasure to meet you. Are you here with someone?"

"No, I'm here on my own," Jenna said.

"Well, it's the luckiest day of my life. Let me get you a drink," he offered.

"Sure," Jenna said and he left her to find the bar.

Elizabeth stood next to her, noticing an old familiar look on her face. "What is it?"

"I have the strangest feeling, like I'm being watched," Jenna said, looking around.

"Sheridan hasn't taken his eyes off you all night." Elizabeth accepted a drink from a waiter.

Jenna shook her head. "No, this is different I can't explain it."

"You're just not used to this kind of attention. Shake it off. Sheridan Stone is a catch, don't let him get away." Elizabeth sipped her drink.

"You're right, time to leave my old life behind, more forward." Jenna said with more bravado than she felt. From the shadow's Rock's brother stared at Jenna.

Scotty excused himself as his phone rang. "Scotty Perelli. How can I help you?"

"It's Rock … I need your help … I'm … in prison, in Turkey."

To be continued….

978-0-595-46499-9
0-595-46499-8

Printed in the United States
91631LV00003B/331-339/A